The Zodiac Detective Justice in the Shadows

Dar

Copyright Page
The Zodiac Detective
Justice in the Shadows
Book #4
© 2024 Daniel Sanjurjo
All rights reserved.

No part of this book may be reproduced, distributed, or transmitted in any form or by any means, including photocopying, recording, or other electronic or mechanical methods, without the prior written permission of the author, except in the case of brief quotations embodied in critical reviews and certain other noncommercial uses permitted by copyright law.

This is a work of fiction. Names, characters, places, and incidents either are the product of the author's imagination or are used fictitiously. Any resemblance to actual persons, living or dead, events, or locales is purely coincidental.

For permissions or inquiries, contact:
dannysanjurnny47@gmail.com

Prologue

Some detectives followed footprints. Leo Maxwell followed patterns.

The dead didn't talk, but they left messages. A turned-over chair, a locked phone, the scent of cigarette smoke lingering too long in an apartment where no one smoked. Clues were never just objects. They were choices. And choices were written in the stars.

Leo stood over the body, hands in his pockets, eyes scanning everything. Adrian Varga. Libra.

The signs were all there. Neat. Orderly. A man who valued balance. The crime scene was anything but.

Furniture overturned. Papers scattered. A crushed red rose on the floor. Deliberate chaos.

It wasn't random. It was a message.

"Looks like a break-in," the officer behind him muttered.

"No." Leo crouched, studying the positioning of Adrian's hands. Still controlled, even in death. He reached out, carefully prying open Adrian's fingers. A crumpled piece of paper was clenched in his grip.

Leo unfolded it.

Justice will find its way.

His pulse ticked up. A Libra's obsession.

This wasn't just a murder. It was about balance. And whoever did this? They understood the game.

Leo smirked to himself. Finally. A worthy opponent.

And he was going to read them like a damn horoscope.

Chapter 1

The morning sun filtered weakly through the heavy curtains of Adrian Varga's high-rise apartment in Prague's Malá Strana district. It was the kind of light that seemed hesitant, as though reluctant to illuminate what lay within. Detective Leo Maxwell stepped inside, his leather shoes clicking softly against the hardwood floor. He paused just beyond the threshold, taking in the scene before him.

It wasn't chaos—it was calculated destruction. Furniture had been overturned, papers scattered across the room like fallen leaves. A single chair lay on its side near the shattered remains of a coffee table, one leg splintered as if kicked violently. The faint smell of smoke lingered in the air, mingling with the metallic tang of blood.

Adrian's body was slumped against the far wall, his head tilted at an unnatural angle. His once-pristine white shirt was now stained crimson, and his glasses rested askew on his face, lenses cracked. There was no sign of forced entry; whoever had done this had been invited in—or known how to bypass security.

Leo crouched beside the body, examining the position of Adrian's hands. They were clenched tightly around something small—a crumpled piece of paper. Carefully, he pried it loose, unfolding it to reveal a hastily scrawled message: *"Justice will find its way."*

He frowned, tucking the note into an evidence bag. Justice? What did that mean? Revenge? Retribution? Or something else entirely?

As he stood, his gaze swept over the room again. Something felt off—not about the violence itself, but about the absence of noise. No screams, no struggle audible enough for neighbors to hear. Whoever had killed Adrian knew exactly what they were doing.

And then there was the rose.

A single red rose lay crushed beneath a toppled vase, its petals scattered like drops of blood across the floor. Leo knelt again, brushing his fingers lightly over the delicate fragments. Why leave a flower? Was it symbolic? A taunt? Or simply a detail meant to distract?

His thoughts drifted momentarily to another crime scene—one from years ago. His sister's lifeless body sprawled in an alley, her killer never caught.

Back then, the police had missed crucial clues because they didn't fit their rigid profiles. Not this time. This time, he would make sure nothing slipped through the cracks.

The sound of heels clicking against the floor broke Leo's concentration. He turned to see a woman standing in the doorway, her notebook clutched tightly in one hand. Her dark hair framed sharp features, and her eyes scanned the room with a mix of curiosity and determination.

"Maggie Hart," she said briskly, extending her free hand. "I'm with *Prague Daily* . I heard you're working this case."

Leo ignored her outstretched hand, instead crossing his arms over his chest. "Private investigation," he corrected. "Not looking for press coverage."

Maggie raised an eyebrow, unfazed by his cold demeanor. "Funny, considering who hired you. Adrian's sister practically begged me to write about this. She thinks you're her last hope."

Leo stiffened. "Then maybe you should focus on writing obituaries instead of interfering."

She smirked, stepping further into the room despite his clear disapproval. "Interfering implies I don't belong here. But since we both want answers..."

Leo sighed, pinching the bridge of his nose. He didn't have time for reporters—especially ones as persistent as Maggie Hart—but arguing with her wouldn't change anything. Besides, she might prove useful. For now.

"What do you know?" he asked finally, keeping his tone clipped.

Maggie flipped open her notebook. "Adrian Varga, thirty-four, software engineer. Brilliant guy, but kept to himself. Rumors suggest he'd been working on some big project lately—something secretive. People close to him say he seemed... distracted."

Leo nodded slowly, filing away the information. Distracted could mean many things, especially for someone born under Libra. Balance was everything to them. Losing equilibrium—even temporarily—could make them vulnerable.

"Libras hate conflict," Leo murmured, more to himself than to Maggie. "If Adrian was stressed, it means someone pushed him too far."

Maggie tilted her head, intrigued. "You really believe all that Zodiac stuff works?"

"It's not 'stuff,'" Leo shot back. "It's behavioral analysis based on patterns. You'd be surprised how often personality traits align with certain signs."

"And yet," Maggie countered, "you're still standing here trying to solve a murder. Patterns won't give us a name."

"They'll give us motive," Leo replied sharply. "Which is more than most investigators bother with."

Their conversation was interrupted by the arrival of a uniformed officer carrying a plastic bag. Inside was a small object wrapped in tissue paper.

"We found this in the trash chute downstairs," the officer explained, handing it over.

Leo unwrapped it carefully, revealing a silver lighter engraved with the initials *AV* . Beneath the initials was a tiny etching of scales—a symbol unmistakably tied to Libra.

Maggie leaned closer, frowning. "Why throw away something so personal?"

"Because whoever did this wanted us to think Adrian threw it away himself," Leo said grimly. "They're playing games."

By the time the forensic team arrived, Leo and Maggie had pieced together several oddities: the cryptic note, the misplaced rose, the discarded lighter.

Each clue hinted at a larger pattern—but none pointed directly to a suspect.

As they left the apartment, Maggie glanced at Leo. "So where do we start?"

Leo hesitated, staring out at the rain-slicked streets of Prague. Somewhere in this labyrinth of cobblestones and shadows, a killer waited. And they weren't going to stop until justice—or vengeance—was served.

"We start with the people

Chapter 2

Leo and Maggie stepped into the sleek, glass-walled conference room of the tech firm where Adrian had worked. Evan Whitmore sat at the head of the table, impeccably dressed in a charcoal suit. His fingers were steepled, his expression composed—too composed.

"Thank you for meeting us," Maggie began. "We're trying to understand what happened to Adrian."

Evan exhaled through his nose, gaze sharp. "It's still hard to believe. Adrian was... complicated, but he didn't deserve this."

Leo studied him. "Complicated how?"

Evan hesitated. "He was brilliant but distant. Always working late, caught up in something. It was like he had one foot in the real world, the other in—" He stopped, reconsidering his words. "Let's just say he had a lot on his mind."

"You mean his project," Maggie interjected. "Something high-stakes."

Evan's lips pressed into a thin line. "If you're suggesting Adrian was involved in something illegal, you're mistaken. But... he was under pressure. He wasn't himself these past few months."

Leo noted the shift in Evan's tone. "Pressure from whom?"

Evan's fingers tapped lightly against the table—a sign of agitation. "I don't know. He didn't talk about it, but I could tell. It was like he was looking over his shoulder."

Maggie leaned in. "Could that have been related to the project?"

Evan hesitated again, then shrugged. "Maybe. He was obsessed with it. Wouldn't shut up about how it could change everything."

"Change everything how?" Leo asked.

Evan forced a tight smile. "I'm not an engineer, Detective. I just know it had potential."

Leo let the silence stretch. Evan was hiding something. Scorpios didn't like to be caught off guard, and right now, Evan looked like a man who had just realized he'd slipped.

"You said Adrian wasn't himself," Leo pressed. "What exactly did you mean?"

Evan's jaw clenched. "He wasn't sleeping. He was paranoid. Told me once that if anything happened to him, the truth would come out anyway."

Leo exchanged a glance with Maggie. "Did he tell you what that truth was?"

Evan's gaze flickered. "No."

The lie was obvious, but pressing too hard now would make him shut down completely. Leo leaned back, changing tactics. "Did Adrian have enemies here? Someone who might have wanted to harm him?"

Evan exhaled sharply. "Clara Novak. Their history was... complicated."

Maggie's eyebrows lifted. "Complicated how?"

Evan hesitated. "She knew how to hold a grudge."

Leo stood, sliding his card across the table. "If you think of anything else, call me."

Evan didn't move to take it. "I already told you everything I know."

Leo didn't believe him.

THE CAFÉ NEAR CHARLES Bridge smelled of fresh espresso and pastries, a stark contrast to the weight in Clara Novak's expression. She arrived late, her dark eyes shadowed, her fingers tightening around the strap of her bag as she slid into the seat opposite Leo and Maggie.

"Thank you for meeting us," Maggie said, offering a small, disarming smile. "We know this isn't easy."

Clara nodded, wrapping her hands around her coffee cup as if drawing warmth from it. "I still can't believe he's gone. Adrian was..." She trailed off, pressing her lips together.

Leo watched her closely. "How close were you?"

A pause. "We had history."

"History?" Maggie echoed.

Clara inhaled slowly. "We worked together. And for a time, we were... involved. But Adrian changed. He started pulling away."

Leo tilted his head. "Why?"

Clara's gaze flickered. "He wouldn't say. Just that it was 'safer this way.' I thought he meant for me, but now..." She exhaled shakily.

Leo noted the tension in her posture. "Did you argue recently?"

Clara flinched—small, but noticeable. "Not exactly."

"Then what?" Maggie pressed gently.

Clara hesitated before speaking. "He was keeping secrets. Not just from me—from everyone. I confronted him about it. He brushed me off."

"Secrets about what?" Leo asked.

Clara shook her head. "His work. The last time we spoke, he told me he'd made a mistake. That he'd trusted the wrong people."

Leo's fingers drummed lightly against the table. "Did he name them?"

"No," Clara whispered. "But I know he was scared."

Maggie glanced at Leo. That matched what Evan had said.

"Clara," Maggie said, keeping her tone gentle, "when we first met, you were hiding something."

Clara's shoulders tensed. "I—"

"The bruise on your wrist," Leo interrupted. "It wasn't from an accident, was it?"

Clara's breath hitched. "I can't—"

"Clara." Leo's voice was quiet but firm. "If someone hurt you, we need to know."

Tears welled in her eyes, but she blinked them away. "The night before Adrian died, I saw someone outside his apartment. A man. He was watching the building."

Maggie leaned forward. "Did you recognize him?"

Clara hesitated. "No... but I think Adrian did."

Leo exhaled slowly. Another piece of the puzzle.

"Why didn't you tell us this before?" Maggie asked.

Clara's voice was barely a whisper. "Because I think he saw me too."

Back at Leo's office, the late afternoon sun cast long shadows across the cluttered space. Stacks of files threatened to topple from every surface, astrological charts covered one wall, and a corkboard, a chaotic web of photos, notes, and red string, dominated another. Maggie paced restlessly, the energy of the city outside a stark contrast to the focused intensity within the room. Leo sat at his desk, his gaze fixed on the corkboard, a half-empty cup of cold coffee forgotten beside him.

"So," Maggie began, breaking the silence, "Evan and Clara. Two very different individuals, both connected to Adrian in... complicated ways. What's your assessment, Leo? Beyond the Zodiac, what's your gut telling you?"

Leo leaned back in his chair, the springs groaning in protest. He rubbed his chin, his eyes still fixed on the board. "Evan... he's a puzzle. Classic Scorpio traits, no doubt. The intensity, the guardedness, the potential for... decisive action, if provoked. He was careful, controlled, almost too polished. Like he was playing a role."

"But?" Maggie prompted, sensing his hesitation. She knew Leo's silences often held as much meaning as his words.

"But," Leo continued, "the crime scene... it felt raw, chaotic. Scorpios, they're planners. They're meticulous. Unless... unless that chaos was a carefully constructed facade. A way to throw us off, to make us look everywhere *but* at him." He tapped a finger against Evan's photo. "Or, to make us look *at* him, but for the wrong reasons."

Maggie nodded, considering this. "And Clara? She's almost the opposite. Openly emotional, seemingly vulnerable..."

"Seemingly," Leo agreed, turning his attention to Clara's photo. "Cancers... they feel deeply. They're protective, intuitive, fiercely loyal to those they care about. But that loyalty... it can be a double-edged sword. If she felt betrayed, abandoned... if Adrian had hurt her..." He didn't need to finish the sentence.

Maggie frowned. "You think she could have been driven to... that? Out of jealousy, or revenge?"

"It's a possibility we can't ignore," Leo admitted. "The emotional intensity is certainly there. But Cancers... they also internalize pain. Killing someone they loved... that would leave deep, visible scars. Her grief seemed genuine, almost overwhelming. But then there's that bruise on her wrist... a small detail, easily dismissed, but..."

"But it doesn't fit," Maggie finished, her journalistic instincts kicking in. "She was hiding something. Maybe not the murder itself, but... something connected to it. Knowledge? Fear? Guilt?"

Leo stood and walked towards the corkboard, his gaze sweeping over the photos, the notes, the connecting threads. "We need to consider all the angles. Evan's potential for calculated misdirection. Clara's emotional depth and possible hidden knowledge. And Adrian... a Libra, caught in the middle, seeking balance, perhaps trusting the wrong person." He tapped Adrian's photo. "The killer exploited that trust, that inherent need for harmony."

Maggie studied the board, the complex web of relationships starting to take shape. "So, we're looking for someone who could manipulate Adrian's desire for peace, someone he wouldn't suspect. Someone close enough to get past his guard."

"Exactly," Leo confirmed. "And both Evan and Clara, in their own ways, fit that profile. But there's something else... something both of them mentioned: Adrian's project. 'Something big,' 'something dangerous.' What if the motive isn't personal at all? What if this is about something far larger? Corporate espionage? The theft of valuable intellectual property?" He paused, a new thought forming. "What if Adrian stumbled onto something he shouldn't have? Something someone was willing to kill to protect?"

Maggie's eyes widened. "We need to understand what Adrian was working on. We need to see what he saw."

As if on cue, Leo's phone buzzed. He glanced at the screen. An anonymous text message:

"Check Adrian's encrypted files. Start with his cloud storage. Password: 'Balance.'"

Leo stared at the message, a mixture of apprehension and anticipation swirling within him. "Someone wants to help us... or lead us into a trap."

Maggie leaned closer, reading the message over his shoulder. "It could be a setup. A way to distract us, or worse."

"Or," Leo countered, a glimmer of determination in his eyes, "it could be the key to unlocking this entire case. We have to follow it. We have to see where it leads." He met Maggie's gaze, a silent understanding passing between them. "We have to be careful."

This expanded version:
*Adds back description.
*Adds internal dialougue and feelings.
*Subtly foreshadows future events.
*Keeps the improvements in dialogue flow from the previous revision.

This should give you a better sense of how to balance streamlining with enriching the narrative. I'll await your feedback before proceeding.

Chapter 3

The café was empty except for the sound of **Leo's fingers tapping against the table.** His coffee had gone cold, untouched. Across from him, Maggie sat hunched over her laptop, eyes scanning endless lines of code.

Adrian's encrypted files. **The last things he tried to protect.**

Leo exhaled. "Tell me you've got something."

Maggie didn't look up. "I cracked the first layer of encryption."

Leo leaned in. "And?"

She frowned. "Most of it's technical data—blueprints, security protocols—but there's one file labeled **'Last Chance.'**"

Leo's pulse quickened. "Open it."

Maggie clicked. The screen filled with a **series of numbers and symbols.**

Leo's brow furrowed. "What is that?"

Maggie shook her head. "It's not a document. It's a location."

She typed furiously, cross-referencing coordinates. A **map appeared.**

A red marker blinked over an address in Žižkov.

Leo's stomach twisted. **Žižkov.**

The district where Adrian **had no reason to be.**

Maggie sat back. "Looks like Adrian was hiding more than files."

Leo grabbed his coat. "Let's go find out why."

DVORAK TECHNOLOGIES' headquarters was a statement – a gleaming tower of glass and steel that dominated the Prague skyline. The lobby was all polished chrome and minimalist design, a space designed to intimidate and impress. As Leo and Maggie stepped inside, they felt a palpable shift in atmosphere, a sense of controlled power.

Maggie, flashing her press credentials, explained they were investigating Adrian Varga's death and needed to speak with Alexander Dvorak. The receptionist, after a moment's hesitation, directed them to the top floor.

Dvorak's corner office was a panoramic vista of the city. The man himself rose from behind a massive desk as they entered, a practiced smile on his face. He exuded charisma, a natural magnetism that Leo immediately associated with Leos. But there was also a calculation in his eyes, a sense of someone who was always several steps ahead.

"Detective Maxwell," Dvorak said, his voice smooth and resonant, extending a hand. "And Ms. Hart, I presume? What brings you to my office?"

Leo bypassed the handshake, getting straight to the point. "We're investigating Adrian Varga's murder. Your name has come up repeatedly."

Dvorak's smile didn't falter, but a subtle shift in his expression betrayed a flicker of... something. Annoyance? Concern? Leo couldn't quite place it. "Adrian's death is a tragedy, of course. But I'm not sure how I can be of assistance."

Maggie stepped forward, notebook in hand. "You and Mr. Varga had a... falling out, years ago. Can you elaborate on that?"

Dvorak sighed dramatically, leaning back in his expensive leather chair. "Ah, yes, the 'infamous split,' as some have called it. It's not uncommon in business. Creative differences, conflicting visions... nothing personal."

"Except it *was* personal," Leo countered, his voice sharp. "From what we understand, Adrian's star was rising, while yours... perhaps not so much. That must have stung." He was probing, testing Dvorak's Leo pride.

Dvorak's jaw tightened, almost imperceptibly, but the smile remained fixed. "Jealousy is not a motivating factor for me, Detective. I've built something far more substantial since then."

Leo studied him, assessing. *Prideful, ambitious, a need to be in control.* Classic Leo traits. If Adrian had threatened Dvorak's position, his reputation... the reaction could have been extreme.

"Tell us about 'Project Phoenix,'" Maggie interjected, watching his face closely for any reaction.

Dvorak's composure flickered, just for a fraction of a second, before he regained control. "I assume you're referring to Adrian's work. We parted ways long before he embarked on that particular venture, so I wouldn't be familiar with the details."

"But you *were* aware of it," Leo pressed. "His encrypted files mention you specifically. Something about exposing vulnerabilities in *your* systems."

Dvorak let out a low chuckle, a dismissive sound, but his eyes had hardened. "If Adrian believed he could somehow undermine me, he was sorely mistaken. I don't respond well to threats."

Maggie and Leo exchanged a quick, meaningful glance. Dvorak wasn't denying involvement; he was deflecting, asserting his dominance.

Before they could push further, Dvorak stood abruptly, signaling the end of the interview. "I sympathize with your efforts, but I have nothing further to add. Now, if you'll excuse me..."

As they were escorted out, Maggie turned to Leo. "Did he do it?"

"He certainly fits a profile," Leo admitted. "A Leo scorned, a reputation threatened... it's a potent combination. But Leos are also careful. The mess at Adrian's apartment... that doesn't feel like his style. It's too... overt."

Maggie nodded thoughtfully. "So, who else benefits from Adrian's death?"

Leo's gaze darkened. "Let's pay Mr. Novotny a visit. Capricorns are less concerned with appearances and more concerned with results."

GREGOR NOVOTNY'S OFFICE was a stark contrast to Dvorak's opulent lair. Located in a quieter district of Prague, it occupied the top floor of an unassuming building, the exterior devoid of any flashy branding. It was a space that reflected practicality and discretion – a Capricorn's domain.

Leo and Maggie were met by a stern-faced receptionist who scrutinized them before allowing them access. Moments later, Novotny himself appeared – a tall, wiry man with sharp features and piercing gray eyes that seemed to assess everything they touched. He exuded a calm, controlled energy, the very embodiment of Capricorn discipline.

"Detective Maxwell," Novotny said, his voice clipped and precise, gesturing for them to enter. "And Ms. Hart. What can I do for you?"

Leo didn't waste time with pleasantries. "We're investigating Adrian Varga's murder. Your name came up in connection with his project."

Novotny raised an eyebrow, settling into his chair behind a minimalist desk. "Indeed. And what exactly have you uncovered?"

Maggie opened her notebook. "We found emails suggesting Adrian offered you exclusive rights to his work – 'Project Phoenix.' Negotiations seem to have stalled. Why?"

Novotny steepled his fingers, his expression unreadable. "Mr. Varga did approach me with a proposal. It was... intriguing, on the surface. However, after careful consideration, I determined the risks outweighed the potential rewards. I advised him to seek funding elsewhere."

Leo leaned forward slightly, studying Novotny's body language. *Capricorns... long-term planners. Methodical. Ruthless when necessary.* "So you declined his offer. Did Adrian take the rejection well?"

Novotny's lips curved into a faint, humorless smile. "Mr. Varga understood my position. He wasn't pleased, naturally, but he respected my decision. Business is business, Detective."

Maggie tapped her pen against her notebook. "We also found a draft email, mentioning a 'final offer.' It suggests negotiations weren't entirely closed."

Novotny glanced at the printout Maggie slid across the desk, then pushed it aside dismissively. "A last-ditch effort on Mr. Varga's part. As I said, I declined."

Leo narrowed his eyes. *Evasion.* "Capricorns value control above all else. If Adrian's project – or Adrian himself – jeopardized that control, you wouldn't hesitate to act."

Novotny's smile vanished, replaced by a steely gaze. "Are you accusing me of something, Detective?"

"Not yet," Leo replied evenly. "But we will need to verify your whereabouts on the night of Adrian's death."

Novotny stood abruptly, signaling the end of the interview. "You'll find I have nothing to hide. Good day."

As they left the office, Maggie turned to Leo. "Is he our guy?"

"He fits a certain profile," Leo admitted. "Capricorns are pragmatic, efficient. They don't act on impulse, but they *do* plan. If Novotny saw Adrian as a liability... he'd remove him. Quietly. Efficiently."

"But?" Maggie pressed, sensing his hesitation.

"But," Leo continued, "something feels... off. Both Dvorak and Novotny had potential motives. But neither of them strikes me as the type to leave behind such a... theatrical crime scene. Whoever killed Adrian wanted us to *notice*. To question everyone, to suspect everyone."

Maggie frowned. "So we're missing something. A piece of the puzzle that doesn't quite fit."

Leo nodded grimly. "We need to go back to Adrian's files. There's more to uncover."

Chapter 4

Leo's office was cluttered with case files, astrological charts, and half-empty coffee cups, the scent of stale caffeine hanging in the air. Maggie sat at his desk, her fingers flying across the keyboard as she sifted through Adrian's encrypted files. The tension between them was palpable—less from argument, more from exhaustion.

"We need to think like Adrian," Leo muttered, rubbing his temples. "If he hid something, he did it in plain sight."

Maggie glanced up. "We already cracked his cloud storage with 'Balance.' What else would he use?"

Leo leaned against the desk, scanning Adrian's notes. "Libras crave symmetry. Harmony. What's a synonym for balance?"

Maggie tapped a few keys, muttering, "Equilibrium."
Nothing.
Leo's jaw tightened. "What about... Justice?"
Maggie typed. The screen blinked—access granted.
She exhaled sharply. "Damn. He was that predictable?"
Leo allowed himself a grim smirk. "Not predictable. Consistent."

Inside the folder, dozens of files appeared—technical blueprints, financial reports, email transcripts. But one file stood out: a video, simply labeled **Final Message**.

Maggie hesitated. "You sure about this?"

Leo clicked play.

Adrian appeared on the screen, the dim light casting deep shadows over his face. His expression was tight, his voice steady but laced with something beneath it. Fear.

"If you're watching this, I'm probably dead."

Maggie's breath hitched.

Adrian continued, his words clipped. **"Project Phoenix… it was supposed to protect people. Instead, I built something that can be weaponized. Someone close to me—someone I trusted—leaked my research. They wanted control, not security."**

Leo leaned in, heart pounding.

"I tried to stop them. I tried to back out. But it was too late. If anything happens to me, look at my last transactions. Follow the money."

The video cut out. The silence that followed was deafening.

Maggie exhaled. "He knew. He knew someone was going to kill him."

Leo's eyes darkened. "And he left us a trail."

Maggie sifted through Adrian's financial records, her mind racing. She had spent years tracing money trails—dirty deals, off-the-books payouts—but this was different. This was personal.

Leo paced the office behind her, his hands shoved into his pockets. "He said to follow the money. What are we missing?"

Maggie's fingers danced across the keyboard. "Most of his transactions are clean—salaries, research expenses, the usual. But here..." She pointed at the screen. "These withdrawals. Large sums, transferred in increments over several weeks. All to an account under the name **Equilibrium Holdings.**"

Leo's pulse quickened. "Equilibrium. There's that word again."

Maggie frowned. "It's a shell company, registered offshore. No real owner listed."

Leo ran a hand over his face. "Someone's laundering money through it. But for what?"

Maggie scrolled further, then stiffened. "Wait. These payments—some of them are linked to another company. **Novotny Solutions.**"

Leo stilled. "Gregor Novotny."

Maggie nodded. "Adrian's 'final offer'—the deal he was pushing? Novotny was involved."

Leo exhaled slowly. **A Capricorn. Pragmatic. Ruthless when necessary.**

"He wasn't just a rival," Leo murmured. "He was part of this from the beginning."

Maggie sat back, rubbing her temples. "So did he kill Adrian? Or did he just pay for it?"

Leo's gaze flicked to the corkboard, the web of red string connecting suspects, motives, and lies. "Novotny wouldn't get his hands dirty. He'd hire someone."

Maggie's jaw tightened. "Then we need to find his killer."

A sharp knock at the door made them both freeze.

Leo exchanged a glance with Maggie before stepping forward. He opened the door—

—and found a single envelope taped to the outside.

Inside was a note, written in perfect, precise script.

"The scales tip soon. Choose wisely."

Leo's blood ran cold.

THE WEIGHT OF ADRIAN'S final message, the chilling reality of an insider betraying him, settled heavily upon Leo and Maggie. They knew they were no longer just investigating a murder; they were unraveling a conspiracy, a web of deceit that reached far beyond the confines of Adrian's apartment.

Before they could delve further into the potential motives of Evan and Clara, Maggie's phone buzzed. It was a text message from one of her contacts, a source she'd cultivated over years of investigative journalism, someone with access to information that wasn't readily available to the public.

"Check Adrian's recent call logs," the message read. "There's a number that appears repeatedly in the days leading up to his death. It's unlisted, but I can trace it if you need me to."

Maggie showed the message to Leo, her eyes alight with a mixture of excitement and apprehension. "This could be it, Leo. This could be our link to the insider."

Leo nodded, his mind already racing. "An unlisted number... someone who didn't want to be identified. Someone who knew Adrian, but didn't want their connection to be known." He paused. "It could be anyone. Dvorak, Novotny, Evan, Clara... or someone we haven't even considered."

"But why call Adrian directly?" Maggie wondered. "If they were leaking information, wouldn't they want to maintain a distance? Wouldn't they use a more... discreet method of communication?"

Leo considered this. "Unless... unless the calls weren't about the leak. Unless they were about something else. A warning? A threat? Or... a final confrontation?"

He looked at Maggie, his expression grim. "We need to trace that number, Maggie. We need to find out who was calling Adrian, and why."

Maggie nodded, already tapping on her phone, sending a message to her contact. "I'll tell him to trace it. It might take some time, but he's good. He'll find something."

While they waited for the trace results, they decided to revisit Clara Novak. The bruise on her wrist, her evasiveness, the raw emotion she'd displayed... it all pointed to something more than just grief.

They found her at her apartment, the same apartment they'd visited before. When she opened the door, her expression shifted from surprise to a guarded wariness.

"Detective Maxwell, Ms. Hart," she said, her voice flat. "What brings you back?"

"We need to clarify a few things," Leo said, his tone firm but not aggressive. "We've been reviewing Adrian's records, and we found something... concerning."

He held up a printout of Adrian's call log, highlighting the repeated calls from the unlisted number. "You told us you hadn't spoken to Adrian recently. But these calls... they tell a different story."

Clara's face paled slightly, but she didn't look away. "I... I may have omitted some details."

"Omitted, or lied?" Maggie asked, her voice sharper now.

Clara hesitated, then sighed deeply, her shoulders slumping. "I was worried. I didn't want to get involved. I didn't want to... believe that someone close to him could have done this."

"So you *did* talk to him," Leo pressed. "What did you talk about?"

Clara's eyes welled up with tears, but this time, they seemed different. Not just grief, but also... fear. "He was scared, Leo. He said... he said he'd made a mistake. That he'd trusted the wrong person."

"Did he say who?" Maggie asked urgently.

Clara shook her head. "No. He wouldn't tell me. He said it was too dangerous. But he... he sounded terrified. I've never heard him like that before."

"And the bruise on your wrist?" Leo asked, his gaze fixed on her arm.

Clara instinctively covered the bruise with her other hand. "It's... it's nothing. I told you, I'm clumsy."

But Leo wasn't buying it. "Clara, if you know something, anything, you need to tell us. Adrian's life was in danger, and whoever killed him... they might still be out there."

Clara hesitated, her internal conflict evident in her eyes. Finally, she spoke, her voice barely a whisper. "The night... the night Adrian died... I saw someone leaving his building. A man. I didn't get a good look at his face, but... he was tall, wearing a dark coat. And he looked... nervous. Like he was trying to get away quickly."

Leo's mind raced. A tall man in a dark coat... it could be anyone. But it was a detail, a small piece of the puzzle that might, just might, lead them to the truth.

"Did you recognize him?" Leo asked.

Clara shook her head. "No. But... there was something familiar about him. Something about the way he moved... I just can't place it."

Leo and Maggie exchanged a look. They were getting closer, they could feel it. But they were also running out of time.

As they are getting closer, the phone buzzed. It was a message from Maggie's contact, a new detail of this mistery.

The message from Maggie's contact arrived like a jolt of electricity, cutting through the tension. She scanned the text, her breath hitching slightly.

"I've got a location," she said. "The unlisted number was traced. It's a burner phone, cash-purchased, but the last known location is an address in Žižkov."

Žižkov. A district where artists and drifters crossed paths with criminals. The streets twisted into dead-ends, perfect for someone who wanted to disappear.

Leo's instincts flared—a silent alarm in his gut. A burner phone meant the caller had taken precautions. This wasn't just someone covering their tracks—it was someone who had planned ahead. Someone who knew how to stay in the shadows.

"We need to go there," Leo said. "Now."

Maggie nodded, already moving. They thanked Clara for her cooperation, though Leo could tell she was still holding something back. He didn't press her—not yet. If she knew more, she'd tell them when she was ready. Or when she had no choice.

The drive to Žižkov was tense, both of them lost in thought. The city lights flickered past, turning the streets into a blur. The address led them to a run-down apartment building on a narrow, unmarked road. The structure sagged under the weight of years, its facade cracked, windows dark.

They checked the address again. It was the right place.

The air was thick with damp concrete and something else—decay. The kind of place where secrets rotted.

Leo pushed the door open cautiously, his hand near his weapon. The apartment inside was nearly empty. Not just in the way of missing furniture—but in the way of missing *life*.

Sparse. Sterile. A threadbare rug, a single unmade bed. No personal belongings. No fingerprints. No sign that anyone had lived here long.

Maggie moved to the small, dented desk in the corner, rummaging through the few items left behind. A half-empty coffee cup. A receipt from a convenience store. An empty cigarette pack. Then she found it—

A discarded phone charger, still plugged into the wall.

"They left in a hurry," she murmured. "Whoever was here—*they knew someone was coming.*"

Leo turned, scanning the space again. Something wasn't right. Not just the lack of belongings, but the *absence of anything traceable.* Whoever had been staying here had wiped the place clean.

A sound from the hallway. A creaking floorboard. A muffled cough.

Leo signaled for Maggie to stay put. He moved toward the door, his steps silent, his breath steady. He peered through the peephole.

An elderly woman stood outside the neighboring apartment, fumbling with her keys. Small. Frail. A face lined with age. She seemed harmless—but Leo knew better than to dismiss anyone.

He opened the door cautiously. "Excuse me, ma'am," he said. "We're with the police. We're looking for the person who lived here."

The woman looked up, startled, her hands shaking. "Police?" Her voice wavered. "What's happened? Is there trouble?"

"We just need information," Leo said, keeping his tone even. "Do you know who lived in this apartment?"

She hesitated. "A young man," she said finally. "He kept to himself."

"Do you know his name?" Maggie pressed.

She shook her head. "No. He never told me. And I never asked."

"When was the last time you saw him?"

The woman frowned, thinking. "A few days ago. Maybe... the night that man was killed. The one in the news. The software engineer."

Leo and Maggie exchanged a look. *The night Adrian was killed.*

"Did you see him leave?" Maggie asked.

"Yes," the woman said. "He was in a hurry. Had a suitcase. He looked... scared."

Leo's pulse quickened. "Scared of what?"

"I don't know." She hesitated. "But he kept looking over his shoulder. Like someone was following him."

Leo leaned in. "Did you see anyone else? Anyone watching him?"

Another hesitation. Then, slowly, she nodded. "A man came earlier that day. Well-dressed. Tall. He looked… important."

Leo's mind immediately conjured two possibilities: *Dvorak* or *Novotny*.

"Did you see his face?" Maggie asked.

The woman shook her head. "It was getting dark. And I didn't want to stare."

Leo exhaled slowly. It wasn't much, but it was something. A connection. A trail.

Maggie's phone buzzed. She glanced at the screen, then back at Leo, her expression unreadable.

"It's my contact," she said. "They traced another number."

She turned the screen so he could read the message:

"Stop digging. You're getting too close."

Leo's jaw tightened. His instincts had been right. They weren't just following a lead anymore.

They were being watched.

MAGGIE LED LEO TO A secluded park bench, far from prying eyes. Her fingers trembled slightly as she opened her laptop.

"I was tracking the phone's digital footprint," she explained, voice tight with urgency. "And then I noticed something… off."

Leo leaned in. "What do you mean?"

"Someone else is watching," she said, pointing at the screen. "This number wasn't just being used to make calls. It was *pinged* multiple times. Someone was tracking Adrian before he died."

Leo's stomach tightened. "Who?"

Maggie ran a trace, her hands moving quickly across the keyboard. A moment later, a name appeared.

Gregor Novotny.

Leo exhaled sharply. "He's not being careful anymore."

Maggie shook her head. "No, he's not."

Before they could react further, her phone

MAGGIE LED LEO TO A secluded park bench, far from prying eyes. Her fingers trembled slightly as she opened her laptop.

"I was tracking the phone's digital footprint," she explained, voice tight with urgency. "And then I noticed something... off."

Leo leaned in. "What do you mean?"

"Someone else is watching," she said, pointing at the screen. "This number wasn't just being used to make calls. It was *pinged* multiple times. Someone was tracking Adrian before he died."

Leo's stomach tightened. "Who?"

Maggie ran a trace, her hands moving quickly across the keyboard. A moment later, a name appeared.

Gregor Novotny.

Leo exhaled sharply. "He's not being careful anymore."

Maggie shook her head. "No, he's not."

Before they could react further, her phone buzzed again. Another message. A new number.

"If you want the truth, come alone."

Leo and Maggie exchanged a glance. The trap had been set. And they were walking straight into it.

Chapter 5

The Vltava shimmered beneath Charles Bridge, the water black and restless under the moonlight. Midnight was the perfect hour for secrets to surface, and Leo Maxwell knew this was a trap.

He just didn't know who had set it.

Lukáš stood at the center of the bridge, hands shoved into his coat pockets, his shoulders hunched as though trying to disappear into the night. A perfect decoy.

Leo was hidden in the shadows near one of the towering statues, his gun resting lightly at his side. Maggie crouched behind a stone column, her camera ready.

They were watching. Waiting.

Then came the footsteps.

Measured. Unhurried.

A tall figure emerged from the far end of the bridge, face obscured by the brim of a hat, moving with deliberate precision. The way he carried himself sent alarms ringing in Leo's mind.

A man used to control.

Capricorn.

JUSTICE IN THE SHADOWS

The figure stopped a few feet from Lukáš. A moment of stillness stretched between them.

Then the man spoke.

"You should have left this alone."

Leo's grip tightened on his weapon. The voice was cold, emotionless. Familiar.

Viktor Havel. Novotny's enforcer.

Lukáš shifted, barely holding his composure. "I—I just want to talk."

Havel tilted his head. "Talk?" He let out a quiet chuckle. "That's not how this works."

Leo saw the movement before Lukáš did—Havel's hand slipping into his coat. A knife? A gun? It didn't matter.

Leo stepped out of the shadows, weapon raised. "Let him go."

Havel turned slowly, his expression calm, like he had been expecting this. "Detective Maxwell." His voice was smooth, unbothered. "I wondered when you'd show yourself."

"No games, Havel," Leo said, his voice like cut glass. "We both know Novotny sent you here."

Havel's lips curved into something that wasn't quite a smile. "Is that what you think?"

Leo's gut twisted. There was something wrong. Too easy. Too clean.

Then he saw it—the reflection of movement in the water below.

Maggie saw it too. "Leo!" she shouted.

Too late.

Two more figures emerged from the shadows, closing in fast. One reached for Lukáš. The other lunged at Leo.

Leo sidestepped, grabbing the attacker's wrist and twisting. A knife clattered to the ground. He slammed his elbow into the man's ribs, sending him sprawling.

Lukáš struggled against the second man, but he was smaller, weaker. The attacker shoved him toward the edge of the bridge—

Maggie moved fast. She hurled a loose cobblestone at the attacker's head. It struck with a sickening crack, and the man staggered.

Leo used the distraction. He turned back to Havel, gun trained. "Call them off."

Havel didn't move. "If you were going to shoot me, Detective, you'd have done it already."

Leo clenched his jaw. He was right. Killing Havel wouldn't get them answers.

Instead, he stepped closer, lowering his voice. "Novotny sent you to clean this up. But you and I both know he's just another puppet."

A flicker of something crossed Havel's face. Annoyance? Amusement?

Leo pressed in. "Who's pulling the strings, Havel? Who's really behind this?"

Silence.

Then, Havel did something unexpected. He smiled.

"Find out for yourself."

Before Leo could react, Havel stepped backward—

—and disappeared into the darkness.

By the time Leo reached the edge, Havel was gone, swallowed by the twisting streets below.

The only thing left behind was a single playing card lying at Leo's feet.

The **Justice** card.

Libra.

Adrian's sign.

A message.

Leo exhaled slowly. **This wasn't over.**

Novotny Solutions' headquarters was cold, clinical. The kind of place built for efficiency, not comfort.

Leo and Maggie were led through silent hallways to a minimalist office where Gregor Novotny sat behind a polished desk, waiting.

He didn't rise. Didn't offer a handshake. Just folded his hands neatly and watched them.

A Capricorn in his element.

"To what do I owe this visit, Detective?" Novotny asked, his voice controlled.

Leo took the seat across from him, locking eyes. "Adrian Varga."

Novotny exhaled softly, as if disappointed. "Ah. That again."

"You worked with him," Maggie said. "And now he's dead."

Novotny's gaze flicked to her, unreadable. "Tragic."

Leo leaned forward. "Tragic? You were paying shell companies linked to his research. You were involved in his project. And now you're acting like he was just another name on your books."

Novotny sighed, adjusting the cuffs of his suit. "Detective, I invest in many projects. Some succeed. Some don't. My hands are clean."

Leo studied him. **Too smooth. Too detached.**

"You expect me to believe you didn't know?" Leo pressed. "That you weren't aware your **own enforcer** was just caught trying to clean this up?"

A muscle in Novotny's jaw twitched. Small, but telling.

"Ah," Leo murmured. "So you do know."

Novotny's expression hardened. "If I were involved, Detective, would I be sitting here entertaining you?"

Maggie raised an eyebrow. "You think that makes you untouchable?"

Novotny smiled slightly. "I think it means you're wasting your time."

Leo watched him carefully. **Capricorns don't bluff. They move only when the outcome is certain.**

Novotny wasn't nervous.

Because he knew something they didn't.

Leo stood. "We'll see."

Novotny simply inclined his head, watching them leave.

As they stepped into the elevator, Maggie exhaled. "That was... pointless."

Leo shook his head. "No. We got what we needed."

Maggie frowned. "Which was?"

Leo glanced back at the glass walls of Novotny's office.

"He's not scared."

Maggie blinked. "And that helps us how?"

Leo's lips pressed into a thin line. "Because whoever **is** behind this? They don't just scare him."

He turned back toward her.

"They own him."

BEFORE LEO COULD REACT, before he could even process the implications of Viktor Havel's presence, the scene erupted in chaos. Viktor pulled a small, metallic device from his coat pocket – a remote trigger.

"You brought friends," Viktor said, his voice still chillingly calm, though a hint of annoyance had crept in. "That wasn't part of the agreement."

A sharp click echoed across the bridge, followed by the whirring of a small engine. From the shadows on either side of the bridge, two figures emerged, their faces obscured by masks, each wielding a weapon – not guns, but something that looked like... tasers. Modified, perhaps, to be even more dangerous.

Maggie, watching the scene unfold, felt the adrenaline spike through her veins. She gripped the cold stone of the statue she hid behind, her breath shallow. Leo's signal hadn't come—he wanted her to stay hidden—but she could see Lukáš trembling, caught between fear and resignation.

"Let him go, Havel," Leo ordered, stepping out of the shadows, his own weapon drawn. His voice was calm but edged with steel. "This isn't about him anymore."

Viktor turned his gaze towards Leo, a flicker of surprise—and then amusement—in his eyes. "Detective Maxwell. Always so... persistent. You think you understand what's happening here? You have no idea."

Leo's mind worked quickly, reading every tic in Viktor's posture, the subtle weight shift, the tell-tale twitch of his fingers. *Virgo. Precision. Order.* If Viktor had backup, they would act without emotion, without deviation.

"Enlighten me," Leo challenged, his eyes locked on Viktor's.

Viktor's smile was thin. "It's about control, Detective. About maintaining order. Adrian Varga... he was a disruptor. He threatened the balance. And balance... must be restored."

There it is again, Leo thought. *Balance.* The Libra's obsession. Twisted into something lethal.

Leo's fingers tensed around the gun. "Who are you working for, Havel? Novotny? Dvorak? Someone else?"

Viktor's smile didn't waver. "Let's just say... I represent certain... interests. Interests that value stability, predictability... and discretion."

"And Lukáš?" Leo asked, gesturing towards the terrified young man. "He's just a pawn, isn't he? Expendable."

Viktor's gaze flicked to Lukáš, then back to Leo. "He made a mistake. He chose the wrong side. And now... he has to pay the price."

Leo took a step forward, placing himself between Viktor and Lukáš. "If you want him, you'll have to go through me."

The smile faded from Viktor's face, replaced by something colder. He raised his hand, fingers poised to signal his masked men.

Before he could, Maggie acted.

With a burst of motion, she launched from behind the statue, hurling a chunk of broken stone at one of the masked figures. The rock struck the man in the temple, dropping him instantly. The second figure whirled, momentarily disoriented—and Leo seized the opening.

He lunged at Viktor, knocking the remote trigger from his hand. They grappled on the cold cobblestones, fists and elbows colliding in the dark. Viktor was stronger, but Leo was faster—and he fought with the quiet fury of a man who had lost too much already.

Maggie sprinted towards the second masked figure, landing a hard kick to his wrist that sent his weapon skittering across the stones. She wrestled him down, securing his hands with a length of rope she had tucked in her bag—always prepared, always thinking ahead.

By the time the scuffle ended, the only sounds were the ragged breathing of the combatants and the distant wail of approaching sirens. Leo stood over Viktor, pinning him to the ground, his arm twisted behind his back.

"It's over, Havel," Leo said, his voice tight with exhaustion and triumph. "You're finished."

Viktor's face was contorted with pain and fury, but his voice remained steady. "You think you've won, Detective? You haven't won anything. You've just... delayed the inevitable."

Leo leaned closer, his breath hot against Viktor's ear. "Then give me a name. Who is the Balance Keeper?"

Viktor's smile returned—a cruel, bloodied curve. "You'll find out soon enough."

Leo's jaw clenched. He looked toward Maggie, who was checking Lukáš for injuries.

"Are you alright?" he asked her.

Maggie glanced up, pale but resolute. "I'm fine. Lukáš?"

Lukáš nodded shakily. "I... I think so. Thank you. Both of you."

Leo exhaled slowly, still holding Viktor down. The night's chill seeped into his bones. He knew the battle was far from over—if anything, they had only peeled back another layer.

Viktor had been a pawn. Now they needed to find the hand that moved him.

The next morning, Leo and Maggie met not in their usual café, but in the hushed sanctuary of a library in Prague's Lesser Town. The high, vaulted ceilings, the towering shelves lined with ancient books, the faint scent of aged paper and leather – it was a place that fostered quiet contemplation, a stark contrast to the digital labyrinth they were navigating.

Maggie spread out a stack of documents on a large, wooden table. The early morning light filtered through the stained glass windows, casting fractured patterns across the polished wood. She pushed a lock of hair behind her ear, dark circles under her eyes betraying how little sleep she had gotten.

"These came in this morning," she said, her voice low, tinged with a mixture of exhaustion and determination. "Financial records, project proposals, client lists... all related to Novotny Solutions. I spent all night digging through them, cross-referencing names, dates, transactions... and something doesn't add up."

Leo leaned over the papers, his sharp eyes scanning the columns of figures, the dense paragraphs of corporate jargon. His mind operated like clockwork—methodical, patient, breaking down the data as if peeling back layers of a human mind.

He traced a finger along the numbers, muttering under his breath. "Capricorns don't leave loose ends... unless they want them to be found."

He stopped suddenly, his finger tapping a specific line item: **Consultation Fees – External Contractors.** The payments were substantial, and they coincided almost perfectly with the timeline of Adrian's death, and with Lukáš's involvement as the information leaker.

Maggie frowned, scribbling notes. "So, Novotny was paying someone off the books. It could be Viktor Havel, acting on Novotny's orders. Or... it could be someone else entirely. Someone even higher up."

Leo leaned closer, his voice almost a whisper. "Someone who operates from the shadows... someone who believes in balance." He glanced at her. "A puppet master."

They began tracing the money through a labyrinth of shell corporations and offshore accounts. Maggie's fingers moved swiftly across her keyboard, accessing encrypted databases through contacts she trusted. Leo watched the maze unfold, his mind filling in the spaces between the numbers.

"They're good," Maggie murmured. "They're really good at hiding things."

Leo's jaw clenched. "Everyone leaves a pattern, no matter how careful they are."

Hours passed. The sun shifted overhead, casting longer shadows across the table. Finally, Maggie's breath caught.

"Here." Her finger hovered over a transaction—small, almost innocuous—funneled into an offshore account under the name **Equilibrium Holdings.**

Leo's breath stilled. The word echoed in his mind.

"Equilibrium... balance... Libra's obsession," he muttered. "The Balance Keeper."

Maggie's eyes widened. "It's them, isn't it? This account... it's the key. But how do we break it open?"

Leo's mind raced. "We need leverage. Direct access. But Novotny won't crack—not without pressure." His brow furrowed. "We're missing something—someone close."

As if on cue, Leo's phone buzzed. The message read: **"Stop chasing shadows. The truth lies closer than you think."**

The cryptic words settled heavily in the quiet library.

Maggie's eyes met his. "Closer... what if we've been looking in the wrong place? What if the truth isn't hidden in offshore accounts or encrypted files? What if it's right in front of us?"

Leo's mind spun, flicking back through every detail—every interview, every profile. Then it clicked.

"Adrian's contacts," he muttered. "Backup files... his safety net. He would've kept something close."

They sifted through Adrian's digital backups until Maggie's breath caught.

"Got it." She opened a folder labeled **Backup Contacts.** Inside was a list of phone numbers—people Adrian had reached out to before his death.

There it was.

Clara's number.

Maggie's voice sharpened. "She lied to us. She told us she hadn't spoken to Adrian recently... but here's the proof."

Leo leaned back, closing his eyes for a moment, mentally piecing Clara's Zodiac profile together. *Cancer. Protective. Emotional. Manipulative when cornered.*

He opened his eyes, cold and steady. "We need to talk to her again. But this time... we break through the shell."

That evening, the air hung heavy as they stood outside Clara's apartment. The building was old, its facade cracked with time. The door creaked open slowly. Clara's eyes widened at the sight of them, surprise flickering into guilt.

"You lied," Maggie said without preamble. Her voice was sharper than before, honed by sleepless nights and rising suspicion. "You told us you hadn't contacted Adrian—but we found your calls."

Clara's hand trembled on the doorframe. "I... I was trying to protect him."

Leo's gaze drilled into her. "Protect him... or control him?"

Clara flinched. Tears welled up in her eyes, but Leo wasn't swayed. He pushed forward.

"What were you trying to warn him about, Clara? What did you hear?"

Her lips trembled. "I overheard Evan... talking to someone on the phone. He mentioned Adrian's project... and something about... 'cleaning house.'"

Leo's pulse quickened. Scorpios always cloaked their actions in shadows. If Evan was involved, he wouldn't leave a trail—he would manipulate others to do the dirty work.

"When was this?" Leo asked softly.

"The day before Adrian died. I didn't think much of it at the time... but now... I think Evan knows more than he's letting on."

Leo's eyes hardened. "He wanted us chasing ghosts while he kept his hands clean. Scorpios thrive on manipulation."

Maggie glanced at Leo, her mind racing. "Then what's our next move?"

Leo's voice was low, steady. "We confront him. But this time... we make him crack."

He paused, his gaze distant.

Maggie touched his arm gently. "Leo?"

He blinked, the shadows in his eyes darker than before. "This case... it's hitting too close to home. I keep seeing her face—my sister's. How I couldn't save her."

Maggie's voice softened. "You didn't fail her, Leo. You're doing everything you can to make sure no one else suffers the same fate."

Leo exhaled slowly, the weight pressing on him visible. He met her eyes, something fragile beneath the hardened exterior.

"I need to believe justice still matters."

Maggie's hand squeezed his arm. "It does. And we'll find it—together."

Chapter 6

The café was nearly empty, the air thick with the scent of burnt espresso. Evan Whitmore sat alone at a corner table, his posture relaxed, his fingers tapping idly against a ceramic cup.

But Leo knew better.

Scorpios didn't relax. They coiled.

Evan looked up as Leo and Maggie approached, his expression unreadable. "Detective Maxwell. Ms. Hart. I had a feeling I'd see you again."

Leo slid into the seat across from him, studying every microexpression. "Let's skip the pleasantries, Evan. You knew Adrian was in trouble. You knew he was being watched. And you said nothing."

Evan tilted his head, an amused glint in his eyes. "If I recall, I said he was distracted. You're the one filling in the blanks."

Maggie leaned in. "You lied to us. You said Adrian was just 'preoccupied,' but Clara overheard you talking about 'cleaning house.' Who were you talking to?"

Evan's jaw tightened, just for a fraction of a second. "Clara always was good at eavesdropping."

JUSTICE IN THE SHADOWS

Leo pressed forward. "The night Adrian was killed, where were you?"

Evan chuckled softly. "Do you actually think I murdered him?" He spread his hands. "Look at me, Detective. Do I seem like the kind of man who gets his hands dirty?"

Leo's fingers drummed lightly against the table. "No. You don't. That's what makes you dangerous."

Evan's smirk faltered.

Scorpios hated being exposed.

Leo leaned closer. "You're not the mastermind, Evan. You're the architect. You set things in motion. You pull the right strings. And if I had to guess? Adrian was a loose end."

Evan's eyes darkened. "That's quite the theory, Detective."

"Not a theory," Leo murmured. "A pattern."

Evan exhaled, his mask slipping just a little. "I told Adrian to walk away. He wouldn't listen."

Maggie's voice was sharp. "So you let him die?"

A pause. Then, Evan's lips pressed together. "I didn't let anything happen."

Leo caught it—the careful phrasing. Not **I didn't do it.** Not **I had nothing to do with it.**

Maggie noticed too. "You knew it was coming."

Evan's gaze flicked to the side, just briefly. Avoidance. Regret?

Or calculation?

Leo set a small evidence bag on the table. Inside, the **Justice** tarot card.

Evan's face betrayed nothing, but his fingers twitched. Recognition.

Leo's voice was quiet. "Who left this?"

Silence.

Then, for the first time, Evan's mask cracked.

"You think you're close, Detective?" he said, his voice lower, colder. "You're not. You're exactly where they want you."

Leo's pulse quickened. **They.**

Maggie frowned. "Who's 'they'?"

Evan stood, adjusting his sleeves, mask slipping back into place. "You should be asking a better question."

He tossed a few bills on the table and turned to leave.

Leo's jaw clenched. "And what's that?"

Evan glanced back, a ghost of a smile on his lips.

"Who's been watching you?"

Then he was gone.

Maggie shivered. "Leo... what if he's right?"

Leo looked down at the tarot card, the word **Justice** staring back at him.

"I think we just stepped into someone else's game."

Leo's office was dimly lit, the glow of his laptop casting harsh shadows. The financial trails, the coded messages, the tarot card—**it all led back to the same place.**

Equilibrium Holdings.

He stared at the screen, heart pounding. He had been looking in the wrong places. **Novotny wasn't the endgame. He was a pawn.**

Maggie's voice pulled him from his thoughts. "Leo. I found something."

She turned her laptop toward him. A **board of directors list.** At first glance, it was unremarkable—shell executives, false names.

But one name stood out.

JUSTICE IN THE SHADOWS 55

Adrian Varga.

Maggie's breath hitched. "Leo... Adrian wasn't just a victim." She swallowed. "He was a part of this."

Leo's pulse hammered. No. That didn't make sense. Adrian had been scared. Hunted.

Hadn't he?

He scanned the documents again. Then he saw it.

A second board member.
One he recognized.
Clara Novak.

The room tilted slightly. Clara. Sweet, heartbroken Clara. The grieving ex. The one who had been **just close enough.**

Maggie whispered, "She lied."

Leo grabbed his coat. "We confront her. Now."

Clara's apartment was dark, the curtains drawn. The scent of vanilla candles lingered in the air, masking something else.

Fear.

She opened the door cautiously, eyes widening at the sight of Leo and Maggie. "Detective...? What's going on?"

Leo stepped inside. "We need to talk."

She folded her arms. "About what?"

Maggie's voice was sharp. "About Equilibrium Holdings."

Clara's breath caught. **There it was.**

Leo kept his tone level. "You were on the board. So was Adrian. Why didn't you tell us?"

Clara swallowed hard. "Because... I didn't think it mattered."

Maggie scoffed. "Didn't matter? Adrian is dead. And you sat there, playing the grieving ex?"

Clara's eyes filled with something that **wasn't guilt.**

It was **anger.**

"You think I wanted this?" she whispered. "You think I wanted him dead?"

Leo studied her. "Then tell us the truth."

Clara's hands trembled, then balled into fists. "Adrian was in over his head. He was supposed to play by the rules, but he got greedy. He thought he could expose them."

Leo's stomach dropped. "Expose who?"

Clara exhaled. "The real Balance Keeper."

Leo's skin prickled. "Who is it, Clara?"

She hesitated. Then—

BANG.

A gunshot.

The window behind Clara **shattered.**

She gasped, her body jerking as blood blossomed across her shirt.

Leo dove forward, catching her as she collapsed. "Clara! Stay with me!"

Her breath came in ragged gasps. "Leo..."

He pressed down on the wound. "Who did this?"

She grabbed his wrist, **fingers ice cold.** Her lips parted—

Then the light faded from her eyes.

Maggie's breath came fast. "Leo—"

Leo turned toward the broken window, heart hammering. The shot had come **from across the street.**

A shadowed figure was already gone.

The mastermind was still out there.

Watching.

Waiting.

Leo clenched his fists.

This wasn't justice.
This was war.

A LIGHT DRIZZLE VEILED Prague as Leo and Maggie met in a small café, the scent of damp earth and brewing coffee filling the air. The previous day's revelations hung heavy between them: Evan's confession of sabotage, the shadowy "Balance Keeper," and the glaring absence of the true mastermind.

"Evan was a tool," Maggie stated, her voice tight with frustration, tracing the rim of her cup. "Used and discarded. Someone else was issuing the commands."

Leo nodded, his gaze unfocused, his mind sifting through possibilities. He considered Novotny, the image of the calculating Capricorn taking shape in his mind. *Long-term strategist. Ruthless when necessary.* The profile fit disturbingly well.

"Novotny has the resources, the network, and the... necessary detachment," Leo murmured, more to himself than to Maggie. "He could easily orchestrate something like this, using individuals like Evan and Viktor as disposable assets."

"But why such an elaborate scheme?" Maggie questioned, her brow furrowed. "Why not simply disable the project discreetly? Why the theatrical crime scene, the cryptic symbols... why the *game*?"

Leo's gaze drifted towards the rain-streaked window, the blurred cityscape reflecting the complexity of the case. "Because Adrian must have discovered something far more significant," he said slowly. "Something beyond mere corporate rivalry. Something Novotny was desperate to keep buried. The murder wasn't just about silencing Adrian; it was a calculated warning. A message to anyone else who dared to investigate."

Maggie's mind raced, processing the implications. "So, what's our next step? A direct confrontation with Novotny?"

Leo shook his head. "Not yet. We lack the irrefutable evidence to link him directly to the murder. We have strong suspicions, yes, but... it's insufficient. We need proof." He paused, his resolve hardening. "For now, we concentrate on Novotny Solutions. We delve into their operations, their clientele, their... vulnerabilities."

The sterile, almost oppressive atmosphere of Novotny Solutions greeted them later that afternoon. They returned under the guise of potential clients, Maggie leveraging her journalistic connections to arrange a meeting, ostensibly to discuss the firm's cybersecurity services. Leo posed as an independent consultant, there to assess their needs – a carefully constructed ruse facilitated by Maggie's network.

Inside, employees moved with an unsettling, robotic precision, their faces bathed in the cool glow of monitors, their fingers dancing across keyboards, manipulating code and algorithms that remained a mystery to Leo and Maggie. The building felt more like a vault, designed to safeguard secrets, than a place of innovation.

They were eventually shown into Novotny's office, the familiar minimalist space. Novotny greeted them with a practiced smile that failed to mask the underlying tension in his eyes.

"Ms. Hart," Novotny said, his voice smooth and controlled, extending a hand. "And Mr. Maxwell. This is... an unexpected visit."

"We're exploring options to strengthen our cybersecurity infrastructure," Maggie explained, adopting a casual, professional tone. "Your firm's reputation precedes it."

Novotny nodded, his expression carefully neutral. "Innovation and security are paramount here. But I suspect your visit is motivated by more than just admiration."

Leo stepped forward, meeting Novotny's gaze directly. "We're also interested in understanding the... larger context of cybersecurity threats," he said, choosing his words carefully. "The risks of data breaches, industrial espionage... and internal vulnerabilities."

Novotny's smile flickered, a brief, almost imperceptible hesitation before he regained his composure. "These are certainly valid concerns in the digital age. But I assure you, we have comprehensive safeguards in place to mitigate such risks."

"Even risks originating from within the company?" Leo pressed, his gaze unwavering.

A muscle in Novotny's jaw tightened subtly. "Internal threats are always a consideration, naturally. We conduct rigorous audits, background checks, and... we swiftly terminate anyone who breaches our stringent security protocols."

Leo and Maggie exchanged a quick, silent communication. They had touched a nerve.

Novotny got up.

As they were leaving, Maggie turned to Leo. "He's hiding something."

"Agreed," Leo replied. "But we are short of proof"

Back at Leo's office, the corkboard, with its growing web of connections, dominated the room. They examined the documents Maggie had acquired – project proposals, client lists, financial records. They also scrutinized Viktor Havel's background, uncovering his history as a freelance "security consultant" with a penchant for... aggressive methods.

"Viktor was more than just Novotny's assistant," Maggie said, a growing unease in her voice. "He was his enforcer. His... weapon."

Leo nodded, his mind piecing together the puzzle. "A Capricorn employing a Virgo. A calculated, efficient, and ruthless combination."

"But who gave Viktor the order to kill Adrian?" Maggie pressed. "And what was the true motive?"

Leo stared at the photos on the corkboard – Adrian, Evan, Clara, Lukáš, Novotny, Dvorak... a constellation of suspicion and intrigue.

"I have a hunch" Leo said.

His phone vibrated. An anonymous text message.

"Time is running out. Choose wisely."

A chill permeated the room, the unseen threat palpable.

Leo met Maggie's gaze, a mixture of frustration and grim determination in his eyes. "We need to uncover the truth about 'Balance Keeper,' Maggie. And we need to do it quickly."

The memory of his sister, the injustice of her unsolved case, fueled his resolve. He wouldn't allow another killer to escape.

The vibrant energy of Prague's Wenceslas Square surrounded them as Leo and Maggie met at a café the next morning, the bustle of city life a stark contrast to the darkness they were confronting. Over coffee, they dissected the previous night's encounter, Viktor Havel's confirmed connection to Novotny, and the growing certainty that Novotny was deeply involved in Adrian's murder.

"Viktor's link to Novotny... it fits," Maggie said, her voice low and thoughtful, idly stirring her coffee. "But it also complicates things. Why would a CEO like Novotny risk such direct involvement? Corporate espionage, even sabotage... those are one thing. Murder is another level entirely."

Leo traced patterns on his cup, his gaze distant, his mind sifting through possibilities. "Unless it's *not* solely about corporate espionage, Maggie. Unless there's a deeper, more significant motive." He considered the Capricorn archetype. "They value control, stability, the long game. If Adrian's project threatened that control, exposed something Novotny desperately needed to keep hidden... extreme measures wouldn't be out of the question."

Maggie frowned, adding notes to her ever-present notebook. "So, what's our next course of action? Do we confront Novotny, accuse him directly?"

Leo shook his head decisively. "Not yet. We still lack the concrete, undeniable proof to connect him directly to the murder. We have strong suspicions, circumstantial evidence, but... it's not sufficient. We need something that will stand up to scrutiny." He paused, his resolve hardening. "For now, we focus on Novotny Solutions. We investigate their operations, their projects, their... concealed activities. We uncover their secrets."

Their strategy involved a carefully planned return to Novotny Solutions. Maggie, leveraging her press credentials, requested an interview with Gregor Novotny, ostensibly for a feature on the company's innovative cybersecurity approach. Simultaneously, Leo, posing as a risk assessment consultant, would conduct a parallel "audit" – a cover story meticulously crafted by Maggie and her network.

The atmosphere inside Novotny Solutions remained eerily sterile, unchanged from their previous visits. Employees moved with a quiet, almost unsettling efficiency, their faces illuminated by the cold glow of monitors, their fingers rapidly typing on keyboards, manipulating complex code and algorithms. The building felt less like a dynamic workspace and more like a secure vault, a place where secrets were fiercely guarded.

They were eventually ushered into Novotny's office, the familiar minimalist space. Novotny greeted them with his usual polished smile, a smile that failed to mask the underlying tension he was undoubtedly experiencing.

"Ms. Hart," Novotny said, his voice smooth and controlled, offering his hand. "And Mr. Maxwell. This is... unexpected. What brings you back?"

"We're preparing an article on the latest trends in cybersecurity," Maggie explained, adopting a casual, disarming tone. "And your company, naturally, is a leader in the field."

Novotny nodded, his expression carefully neutral. "We pride ourselves on our innovative solutions. But I suspect your visit is driven by more than just journalistic interest."

Leo stepped forward, meeting Novotny's gaze directly. "We're also interested in understanding the challenges confronting the industry," he said, choosing his words with precision. "The growing sophistication of cyber threats, the risk of data breaches... the potential for vulnerabilities from within."

Novotny's smile flickered, a brief, almost imperceptible crack in his composure before he regained control. "These are certainly valid concerns. But I assure you, we have comprehensive security measures in place to mitigate all potential threats."

"Even threats originating from within your own organization?" Leo pressed, his gaze unwavering.

Novotny's jaw tightened subtly. "Internal threats are always a consideration, Mr. Maxwell. We conduct thorough background checks, regular security reviews, and... we swiftly terminate anyone who violates our strict confidentiality policies."

A sign.

Before anything.

He got up.

Outside, Maggie to Leo. "He's nervous."

"I agree," Leo replied grimly. "But the evidence?"

Later that evening, the dim light of Leo's office illuminated the stacks of documents Maggie had managed to acquire – project summaries, client lists, internal memos. They also focused on Viktor Havel, scrutinizing his background, his previous employment, his connections.

"Here, Leo," Maggie said, pointing to a detail in Viktor's file. "Before Novotny Solutions, he worked as a freelance 'security consultant.' But it's more than that... his specialty was data retrieval, digital forensics... and sabotage."

Leo leaned in, his eyes narrowing. "A hired gun. A digital assassin. That explains his proficiency in accessing Lukáš's cloud storage, his ability to erase his tracks so effectively."

"But who issued the order?" Maggie pressed. "Who directed him to target Adrian?"

A thought.

Leo stared at the corkboard, at the interconnected photos – Adrian, Evan, Clara, Lukáš, Novotny, Dvorak... a web of deceit, suspicion, and violence.

"We're getting closer, Maggie," he said finally, his voice low and serious. "But we're also in greater danger. The closer we get to the truth, the more desperate they'll become. And they've already demonstrated their willingness to do anything to protect their secrets." He paused, his gaze meeting Maggie's, a flicker of vulnerability in his eyes. "They've been manipulating us, Maggie. From the start. Controlling the information, leading us astray."

His sister, again.

"I won't let it happen again," he said, his voice raw with emotion. "I won't let another killer walk free."

"You won't," Maggie assured him, her voice firm and resolute. "We won't let them. We're in this together, and we'll uncover the truth, no matter the cost."

Chapter 7

The bullet that killed Clara still felt hot in Leo's hands. She had died **with the answer on her lips.**

And the killer was still watching.

Leo and Maggie sat in his car, parked outside a desolate warehouse in Prague's industrial district. Rain dripped down the windshield, washing the city in streaks of neon light. The address had been tucked in Adrian's encrypted files, buried under false business fronts.

Equilibrium Holdings had been a **distraction.** A shell. A front for something deeper.

The real **Balance Keeper** was inside.

Maggie reloaded her gun. "We should call backup."

Leo's grip tightened on the wheel. "We don't have time."

Maggie exhaled sharply. "Leo—"

"She died in my arms, Maggie," Leo said, voice like stone. "I'm not letting them walk away."

Maggie studied him, then nodded. **They were in this together.**

Leo reached under his seat, pulling out a compact shotgun—something he'd stashed years ago for nights like this. He chambered a shell.

They weren't leaving until this was over.

The warehouse smelled of **old metal and gasoline.** Shadows stretched across rusted machinery, gears frozen in time.

Leo moved like a ghost, Maggie at his back.

The floor creaked beneath their boots. **Someone was here.** Watching. Waiting.

Then—

A voice echoed from the darkness.

"You should have stopped digging, Detective."

Leo turned toward the source. A **figure emerged from the shadows**, stepping into the dim light.

Gregor Novotny.

But he wasn't alone.

Behind him, four armed men.

Novotny smiled. "Justice, balance... they're just words. The world runs on power, Leo. And you're about to learn that the hard way."

Leo didn't hesitate.

He fired.

The first blast took one of the guards in the chest—**he went down before he could scream.**

Maggie pivoted, putting two rounds into another before he could raise his weapon.

The warehouse **erupted.**

Gunfire tore through the machinery, sparks flying. **Leo and Maggie dove behind a rusted conveyor belt, bullets shredding metal where they had stood.**

Leo gritted his teeth. **They were outnumbered.**

Maggie reloaded. "Tell me we have a plan."

JUSTICE IN THE SHADOWS

Leo peeked out. **Three guards left. Novotny watching.**

"We split them up," Leo muttered. "You draw them left. I'll take the high ground."

Maggie nodded, then—**she was running.**

Gunfire chased her, but she was fast, darting behind pillars, forcing two of the men to break away.

Leo **climbed the old machinery**, boots silent on metal. The third gunman turned—

Leo dropped down, slamming the shotgun against his skull.

The man collapsed, his weapon clattering.

Then it was **just Novotny.**

Leo turned, leveling his gun.

The businessman **stood still, unarmed.**

Rain leaked through the warehouse ceiling, dripping onto his expensive suit.

"You always were predictable, Maxwell," Novotny sighed.

Leo's finger hovered over the trigger. "You killed Adrian."

Novotny smiled. "No, Detective. **I gave the order.**"

Leo clenched his jaw. **Cold. Unapologetic.** Capricorns never moved unless they were certain they would win.

And Novotny **was still standing here.**

Why?

Maggie's voice cut through the silence. "Leo—"

A sound **behind him.**

Leo turned too late.

A knife slashed across his ribs.

Pain **exploded** through his side.

The attacker—**Viktor Havel.**

Blood dripped from the blade.

Leo **staggered, but didn't fall.**

Havel **smiled.** "Justice, Detective?" He twisted the knife in his grip. "That's a fairy tale."

Leo's **gun came up.**

BOOM.

Havel's smile vanished.

A **bullet tore through his chest.**

He collapsed, gurgling, his knife clattering to the floor.

Leo turned back to Novotny—

But **he was running.**

Maggie fired, **barely missing.**

Leo **pushed through the pain**, chasing Novotny up an old steel staircase. His vision blurred, but he forced himself forward.

Novotny reached the top—**a catwalk leading to an exit.**

Leo **fired.**

The bullet **shattered Novotny's knee.**

The man **screamed, collapsing against the railing.**

Leo closed the distance, panting, blood soaking his side.

Novotny groaned, trying to crawl away. "You... you can't stop it."

Leo grabbed him by the collar, yanking him up. "Stop what?"

Novotny coughed blood. "Balance isn't one person, Maxwell." His eyes gleamed. **"It's a system."**

Leo's grip tightened. "Then consider this a system failure."

He shoved Novotny **over the railing.**

The man's **scream was lost in the storm.**

He hit the ground **with a sickening crunch.**

Silence.

Leo **stood over the edge, breathing hard.**

Maggie approached, gripping his arm. "Leo. It's done."

Leo wiped blood from his mouth. **"Not yet."**

He reached into Novotny's jacket.

A **phone.**

A single message on the screen.

UNKNOWN NUMBER: *Tell me when it's finished.*

Leo's stomach turned.

Someone else was still out there.

Watching.

Waiting.

Maggie read the message, exhaling. "It never ends, does it?"

Leo stared into the rain. **His sister's case had never ended. Now Adrian's wouldn't either.**

But tonight?

Tonight, **they had burned the system to the ground.**

Leo exhaled. "For now... it's enough."

Maggie nodded. "Let's go home."

And as sirens howled in the distance, Leo **let the rain wash the blood away.**

For now.

Dawn crept over the Prague skyline as Leo and Maggie hunched over Adrian's recovered cloud data, their faces illuminated by the glow of the monitor. They were searching for any overlooked connection to Novotny Solutions, any digital breadcrumb that might lead them closer to the truth. The encrypted files were a tangled web, but Maggie, with a sudden gasp, found something.

"These emails..." she said, her voice rising with a mixture of urgency and disbelief, "they're between Adrian and someone using the alias 'Project Oversight.' They're dated just days before his death."

Leo peered over her shoulder, his eyes scanning the contents. The emails revealed a heated exchange – Adrian accusing the anonymous sender of misusing confidential information related to Project Phoenix.

Leo's jaw tightened. The meticulous planning, the careful control... it all resonated with a chilling familiarity. *Novotny*. He could almost visualize the man, a spider at the center of his web, each strand meticulously placed. "If Adrian threatened to expose him..." he trailed off, the implication hanging heavy in the air.

"But why not simply sabotage the project directly?" Maggie wondered, her brow furrowed in thought.

"Because that's not how a mind like his operates," Leo replied, a hint of grudging respect in his voice. "It's not just about silencing Adrian; it's about the *message*. The slow, deliberate dismantling of his life." He thought of the Capricorn archetype – the calculated strategist, the master of the long game.

Before they could explore this further, Maggie's phone vibrated. An anonymous text: "The truth is closer than you think. Look to the stars."

Maggie showed the message to Leo, her expression a mixture of confusion and annoyance. "Another cryptic Zodiac reference? Is this a game to them?"

"Someone's toying with us," Leo mused, his fingers drumming lightly on the table. "Using the Zodiac as a distraction... or perhaps as a twisted form of guidance."

"Or... maybe they're genuinely trying to help," Maggie suggested, a flicker of hope in her voice. "What if 'look to the stars' is literal? Referring to someone's astrological sign?"

Leo's gaze sharpened. Novotny's calculated nature made him the prime suspect, but a nagging doubt persisted. "Is there another player we've overlooked? Someone hiding in plain sight?"

The afternoon found them seeking out Lukáš Horák, hoping he could shed light on the mysterious "Project Oversight" alias. At his safehouse, Lukáš greeted them with a visible tremor, his hands shaking as he clutched a cup of tea.

"You've discovered something," he stated, his voice a low murmur, his eyes darting nervously between their faces.

"We have," Maggie confirmed, showing him the printed emails. "Do you recognize this account?"

Lukáš hesitated, then nodded slowly. "It... it's the same alias I used. For the information leak. But I stopped, I swear, after Adrian confronted me."

Leo studied him intently, his mind sifting through observations. The careful phrasing, the averted gaze, the underlying anxiety... *Virgo under pressure*. The guilt was palpable, but was it the complete story? "Did anyone else have access to your account?"

"No," Lukáš insisted, then paused, his voice dropping to a near whisper. "But... someone *knew* about it. Someone approached me... after Adrian's death."

"Who?" Maggie pressed, her voice sharp and insistent.

Lukáš swallowed hard. "Novotny. He said... he could offer me protection. If I cooperated."

A silent exchange passed between Leo and Maggie. The puzzle pieces were beginning to fall into place, forming a disturbing picture.

"He's playing a double game," Leo stated, his voice grim. "Exploiting Lukáš's vulnerability while simultaneously covering his own tracks."

"But why frame us?"

Leo had a thought.

Leaving Lukáš's safehouse, Maggie voiced the question that had been nagging at her. "We need irrefutable proof. Something that definitively links Novotny to Adrian's murder."

"I know," Leo replied, his gaze fixed on some distant point. "And I believe I know where we might find it."

The evening found them back at Adrian's apartment, the scene of the crime. Despite previous forensic sweeps, Leo felt a persistent intuition, a sense that a crucial piece of evidence remained hidden.

"There *will* be something," he murmured, his eyes meticulously scanning the room. "Something personal. A subtle signature."

Maggie nodded, joining the search. They moved through the disarray, a silent partnership forged in their shared pursuit of justice. It was Maggie who spotted it – a faint glint of metal beneath the sofa, partially obscured by dust. A small USB drive.

"What's this?" she asked, holding it up for Leo to see.

Leo took the drive, turning it over in his hands. "Let's find out."

Back in the familiar confines of Leo's office, the drive relinquished its secrets. Encrypted messages between Novotny and an unidentified individual discussing Adrian, financial records tracing to offshore accounts, and, most damningly, a recording of Novotny admitting to orchestrating the sabotage.

"This is it," Maggie breathed, a tremor of excitement in her voice. "This proves his involvement."

"Involvement, yes," Leo corrected, his expression still grave. "But not necessarily *guilt*. The strings could still lead higher."

Maggie frowned. "You suspect Dvorak?"

"It's a strong possibility," Leo conceded. The delegation of responsibility, the manipulation from a distance... it aligned with a pattern. *The need for absolute control, but exercised indirectly.*

As darkness enveloped the city, a quiet tension settled between them. Leo withdrew, his usual intensity replaced by a haunted stillness. Maggie sensed the shift, waiting patiently until they were alone.

She spoke softly.

Leo, met her gaze. The betrayals inherent in this case... they resonated deeply, a painful echo of a wound that had never fully healed.

She got closer to him.

His eyes still on hers.

"It's not," Maggie assured him, her voice firm and unwavering. "And we *will* find it. For Adrian, and for everyone who deserves justice. Including you." Her words were a promise, a shared commitment to a cause that transcended the personal.

THE AIR INSIDE GREGOR Novotny's office was thick with a controlled stillness, a stark contrast to the bustling energy of the open-plan workspace just beyond the door. Employees moved with a quiet, focused efficiency, their screens displaying a mesmerizing dance of code and data. The space felt less like a creative environment and more like a carefully guarded vault.

Novotny greeted them with a polished smile that didn't quite reach his eyes, a mask of composure. *Classic Capricorn*, Leo thought, observing the man's controlled demeanor.

"Back so soon?" Novotny inquired smoothly, gesturing for them to sit. "Have you reconsidered my lack of involvement?"

Leo ignored the subtle provocation, placing the USB drive on the gleaming surface of Novotny's desk. "We recovered this from Adrian's apartment. Perhaps you could explain its contents."

The smile flickered, a brief, almost imperceptible tremor before Novotny regained his composure. His voice remained even. "I've no idea what that is. I've never seen it before."

Maggie leaned forward, her voice sharp and direct. "It contains encrypted communications between you and an unidentified individual, discussing Adrian's project. Financial records linking to offshore accounts. And a recording – your own voice, Mr. Novotny – admitting to orchestrating the sabotage."

A muscle in Novotny's jaw twitched, a brief, involuntary betrayal of his inner turmoil. He recovered quickly. "Even if that were authentic, it doesn't prove I murdered him."

"No," Leo agreed, his voice low and steady. "But it establishes a clear motive – and the means to execute it."

The afternoon found them at Alexander Dvorak's headquarters, a space that, in stark contrast to Novotny's stark minimalism, exuded an aura of opulent power. Plush leather furniture, gleaming gold accents, and the faint scent of cedarwood created an atmosphere of established authority.

Dvorak, the quintessential Leo, received them with a confident, almost regal bearing. His posture radiated control.

"To what do I owe this unexpected visit?" he asked, leaning back in his imposing chair.

Leo met his gaze directly. "We're investigating your connection to 'Balance Keeper.' Your collaboration with Novotny. And Adrian's sabotage."

Dvorak raised a perfectly sculpted eyebrow, seemingly unfazed. "Those are rather ambitious accusations. Do you have any evidence to substantiate them?"

Maggie slid the USB drive across the expansive desk. "This should be sufficient. Encrypted messages, financial trails, recordings – it's all there."

The confident smirk vanished from Dvorak's face, replaced by a cold, calculating glint in his eyes. "Even if that were genuine, it doesn't implicate *me* in a murder. You're chasing shadows."

Leo leaned forward, his voice a low, intense murmur. "A Leo rarely acts without a deliberate purpose. Killing Adrian wasn't just about silencing him; it was a calculated statement. A demonstration of power."

A flicker of something – perhaps acknowledgement, perhaps irritation – crossed Dvorak's face before he shrugged dismissively. "Perhaps. Or perhaps you're reading too much into this. In any case, circumstantial evidence won't be enough to connect me to the crime."

Outside Dvorak's office, Maggie turned to Leo, her voice filled with a mixture of frustration and uncertainty. "Do you believe either of them is the actual killer? Or are they both acting as shields for someone – or something – else?"

"It's certainly a possibility," Leo admitted. "A Capricorn, like Novotny, values meticulous planning and efficiency – often utilizing intermediaries to carry out their plans. And a Leo, like Dvorak, craves control – orchestrating events from a position of power, but maintaining a safe distance."

"But why frame Lukáš?" Maggie pressed. "Why leave those deliberately misleading clues, like the scales?"

"It's a calculated game," Leo said, a darkness creeping into his voice. "A deliberate attempt to create confusion, to make us question everyone – even ourselves. To keep us off balance."

Back in the dim light of Leo's office, they reviewed the accumulating evidence that evening. Maggie arranged photos of Novotny and Dvorak on the corkboard, connecting them with red string to the other individuals involved, a visual representation of the complex web of relationships.

"So, is Novotny the strategist, and Dvorak the enforcer?" Maggie mused, tapping a finger against her chin.

"Not necessarily," Leo countered. "Capricorns are meticulous planners, but they also understand the value of delegation. Dvorak could have acted independently – or been manipulated into taking the fall."

Maggie frowned. "Either way, we're still missing a critical element. A key piece of the puzzle."

Before they could delve further into their analysis, Leo's phone vibrated. Another anonymous text: "The scales tip soon. Choose wisely."

Maggie read the message over his shoulder, her brow furrowed with concern. "What does that even mean?"

"It means our time is rapidly diminishing," Leo replied, his voice grim. "Whoever is sending these messages is planning something – and we're standing directly in their path."

A heavy silence settled between them, the unspoken tension amplified by the weight of the case. Maggie noticed Leo's increasing withdrawal, his usual sharp focus clouded by a shadow of past trauma. When they were finally alone, she spoke softly.

"This case is stirring up painful memories for you, isn't it?" she asked gently. "Memories of your sister."

Leo hesitated, visibly startled by her perceptiveness. "Cases like this... where trust is so completely violated... they inevitably bring it all back," he admitted, his voice raw with emotion. "The feeling of helplessness. My failure to protect her."

Maggie gently placed a hand on his shoulder, a gesture of quiet support and understanding. "You're not failing now, Leo. You're doing everything you can. For Adrian, for Lukáš, for the very principle of justice."

For a fleeting moment, Leo allowed his carefully constructed defenses to crumble, revealing the raw, enduring pain beneath. "I just... I need to believe that justice is still possible. That it's attainable."

"It *is*," Maggie affirmed, her voice strong and unwavering. "And we'll achieve it – for Adrian, for your sister, and for everyone who has been wronged. We'll find the truth, together." Her words were a pledge, a shared commitment to a cause that transcended the personal, a beacon of hope in the gathering darkness.

Chapter 8

The morning sun, fractured by the ornate window of the café, cast shifting patterns on the table as Leo and Maggie met. The bustle of Charles Bridge was a distant hum, a counterpoint to the quiet intensity of their discussion. They reviewed the evidence, the tangled threads connecting Novotny Solutions and Dvorak Technologies, seeking the definitive link to Adrian's murder.

"Novotny orchestrated the sabotage," Maggie stated, her voice low, tracing the rim of her coffee cup. "But he wouldn't act alone. Someone above him was issuing the orders."

Leo nodded, his gaze distant, his mind already constructing a profile of Dvorak. *Leo.* The inherent pride, the ambition, the drive for dominance... it all pointed to a capacity for ruthless manipulation. He could see Dvorak, viewing Adrian's project as a challenge to his own carefully constructed empire, using Novotny as a disposable instrument.

"Dvorak fits the behavioral profile," Leo agreed, his voice a thoughtful murmur. "He has the ego to demand absolute control, but also the calculated detachment to avoid direct involvement. He wouldn't get his hands dirty, but he wouldn't hesitate to orchestrate the chaos from afar."

"But why Novotny?" Maggie questioned, tapping a pen against her notebook. "Why not eliminate the threat directly?"

"Because Leos, especially those in positions of power, are acutely aware of appearances," Leo explained. "Using an intermediary provides a layer of protection. Plausible deniability. He can distance himself from any negative consequences."

Maggie frowned, her mind working through the implications. "So, what's our next move? Do we confront Dvorak directly?"

"Not yet," Leo replied decisively. "We need more than a strong suspicion based on his personality. We need irrefutable proof linking him to Adrian's murder. Our immediate focus should be Dvorak Technologies – we need to uncover any connection to 'Balance Keeper.'"

The sleek, almost sterile interior of Dvorak Technologies greeted them later that afternoon. They posed as potential investors, interested in the company's cybersecurity innovations. Maggie, leveraging her press credentials, had secured a tour of the facilities, while Leo, playing the role of an independent consultant, requested an audit – a carefully crafted deception facilitated by Maggie's network.

Inside, employees moved with a quiet, almost unsettling precision, their attention seemingly glued to the glowing screens before them. The space felt less like a collaborative environment and more like a heavily guarded fortress.

When they were finally ushered into Dvorak's office, the man himself grected them with a polished smile that failed to mask the underlying assessment in his eyes. *The Lion, sizing up his audience*, Leo observed, noting Dvorak's controlled demeanor, the subtle cues of a Leo's calculated charm.

"Ms. Hart," Dvorak said, his voice a smooth baritone, extending a hand. "And Mr. Maxwell, I understand? What brings you to my domain?"

"We're exploring current trends in cybersecurity," Maggie replied, maintaining a neutral, professional tone. "Your company has certainly established a formidable reputation."

Dvorak acknowledged the compliment with a slight nod, a flicker of something unreadable in his eyes. "Innovation is our driving force. But I suspect your interest extends beyond mere industry observation."

Leo stepped forward, his gaze unwavering. "We're also interested in exploring potential collaborations – specifically, between Dvorak Technologies and Novotny Solutions. Any insights you might share would be invaluable."

The polished smile wavered, a subtle shift in Dvorak's composure. He quickly regained his control. "Novotny and I have partnered on various ventures over the years. Standard industry practice."

"Including any related to Adrian Varga?" Maggie interjected, her voice taking on a slightly sharper edge.

A muscle in Dvorak's jaw tightened, a brief, involuntary betrayal of his inner state. "Adrian's work was undeniably groundbreaking, but ultimately flawed. I personally cautioned him about the inherent risks."

Leo and Maggie exchanged a quick, knowing glance. They had touched a nerve.

Before they could pursue this line of questioning, Dvorak rose abruptly, effectively terminating the meeting. "If you'll excuse me, a prior engagement requires my attention. My assistant will escort you out."

Outside Dvorak's office, Maggie turned to Leo, her voice low and urgent. "He's definitely concealing something."

"Without question," Leo agreed, his expression grim. "But we still lack concrete evidence. Our next step is to delve deeper into their partnership – and expose the truth about 'Balance Keeper.'"

Later, in the familiar, cluttered sanctuary of Leo's office, they pored over the documents Maggie had acquired through her network. Among them, a series of emails detailing a joint venture between Dvorak Technologies and Novotny Solutions – the project codenamed "Balance Keeper."

"This could be the key," Maggie whispered, her voice filled with a mix of excitement and apprehension. "If we can definitively link this project to Adrian's murder, we'll have him."

"But how do we establish that link?" Leo countered, his voice laced with frustration. "Without direct proof, it's all circumstantial, easily refuted."

Maggie paused, considering their options. "Perhaps it's time for a calculated gamble. We confront Dvorak – present him with this information. Force him to react, to reveal something."

Leo shook his head, his expression firm. "That's far too risky. He's already demonstrated a willingness to eliminate perceived threats. We need a different strategy. Something less direct." He tapped a finger on the photo of Dvorak. *Leo. Proud. Image-conscious.*

Before their next strategy session could begin, Leo's phone vibrated. Another anonymous text: "The scales tip soon. Choose wisely."

Maggie read the message over his shoulder, a knot of worry tightening in her chest. "What does that even mean?"

"It means our window of opportunity is closing," Leo replied, his voice heavy with a sense of impending urgency. "Whoever is sending these messages is about to make a move – and we're caught in the middle."

The weight of the case, the constant pressure, began to take its toll. Maggie noticed Leo withdrawing into himself, his focus shifting inward. When they were alone, she spoke softly, her voice filled with concern.

"This is bringing back memories, isn't it?" she asked gently. "Memories of your sister."

Leo hesitated, caught off guard by her insight. He turned away, staring out the window at the city lights. "Cases like this… where trust is so completely violated… it's hard not to think of her," he admitted, his voice raw with emotion. "Of my inability to protect her."

Maggie gently placed a hand on his arm, a gesture of quiet support. "You're doing everything you can now, Leo. For Adrian, for Lukáš, for the very concept of justice. Don't let the past paralyze you."

For a brief moment, Leo's defenses wavered. "I just… I don't want to experience that kind of failure again."

"You won't," Maggie said, her voice filled with a quiet strength. "Not while we're working together. We'll find the truth." Her words were a promise, a shared commitment to a cause that transcended their personal struggles.

"

Driven by a renewed sense of urgency, Leo and Maggie returned to Adrian's digital archive, seeking any overlooked connection to "Balance Keeper." The encrypted files were a daunting maze, but Maggie, with a sudden exclamation, discovered something crucial.

"Look at these," she said, her voice tight with a mixture of urgency and disbelief. "Emails between Adrian and someone using the alias 'Project Oversight.' They're dated just days before he was killed."

Leo leaned closer, his eyes quickly scanning the content. The emails contained a heated exchange – Adrian accusing the anonymous sender of misusing confidential information related to Project Phoenix.

A muscle in Leo's jaw tightened. The meticulous orchestration, the careful control... it all pointed to a familiar pattern. This felt like Dvorak's influence, not Novotny's. *Leo.* The inherent need for dominance, the potential for ruthlessness when threatened... "If Adrian posed a threat to his power, his carefully constructed world..." he murmured, the implication hanging heavy in the air.

"But why such an indirect, elaborate approach?" Maggie wondered, her brow furrowed in thought. "Why not simply terminate the project?"

"Because a Leo, especially someone like Dvorak, doesn't just react; he makes a *statement*," Leo explained, a glimmer of understanding in his eyes. "It's not solely about silencing Adrian; it's about demonstrating power. About controlling the narrative." He envisioned Dvorak as a puppeteer, manipulating events from a distance, relishing the unfolding chaos.

Their discussion was interrupted by the vibration of Maggie's phone. Another anonymous text: "The truth is closer than you think. Look to the stars."

Maggie showed Leo the message, her expression a mix of frustration and confusion. "Another cryptic Zodiac message? Is this some kind of game?"

"Perhaps," Leo mused, his fingers tapping a thoughtful rhythm on the table. "Or perhaps someone is attempting to guide us, in their own unconventional way. Using the Zodiac as a... code."

"Or maybe it *is* a genuine attempt to help," Maggie offered, a sliver of hope in her voice. "Could 'look to the stars' be a literal instruction? Pointing to someone's astrological sign?"

Leo's gaze sharpened. Dvorak, the obvious Leo, was the primary suspect, but a persistent nagging doubt remained. "Is it possible there's another player involved? Someone we haven't fully considered?"

Hoping to shed light on the "Project Oversight" alias, they decided to revisit Lukáš Horák that afternoon. At his safehouse, Lukáš greeted them with a visible tremor, his hands shaking as he clutched a cup of tea.

"You've found something," he stated, his voice a low, nervous murmur, his eyes darting between them.

"We have," Maggie confirmed, showing him the printed emails. "Do you recognize this account?"

Lukáš hesitated, then nodded slowly. "It's... it's the same alias I used. When I leaked the data. But I swear, I stopped after Adrian confronted me."

Leo studied him intently, observing his behavior through the lens of his astrological understanding. *Virgo.*

Detail-oriented, adaptable, but also prone to anxiety and guilt when under pressure. "Did anyone else have access to your account?"

"No," Lukáš insisted, then paused, his voice dropping to a near whisper. "But... someone *knew* about it. Someone approached me... after Adrian died."

"Who?" Maggie pressed, her voice sharp and insistent.

Lukáš swallowed hard. "Dvorak. He said... he could protect me. If I cooperated."

Chapter 9

A look of grim understanding passed between Leo and Maggie. The puzzle pieces were falling into place, creating a disturbing image.

"Dvorak's playing a complex game," Leo stated, his voice hard. "Using Lukáš as a pawn, while simultaneously diverting suspicion from himself."

"why Lukáš?" Maggie asked.

"to protect himself" Leo said.

The need for concrete evidence pressed upon them as they left Lukáš's safehouse. "We need something undeniable, Leo," Maggie said, her voice filled with urgency. "Something that directly links Dvorak to Adrian's murder."

"I know," Leo replied, his gaze distant, focused. "And I have a feeling where we might find it."

A sense of foreboding settled over them as they returned to Adrian's apartment that evening, the scene of the crime. Despite previous forensic examinations, Leo felt a persistent intuition, a belief that a crucial piece of evidence remained hidden.

"A Leo, even in crime, might leave a subtle trace," Leo murmured, his eyes scanning the room with meticulous care.

"A touch of ego, a behavioral signature." He wasn't looking for obvious clues, but for something reflecting Dvorak's personality.

Maggie nodded, joining the search. They moved through the disarray, a silent, synchronized effort. It was Maggie who made the discovery – a faint glint of metal beneath the sofa, partially hidden by dust. A small USB drive.

"What's this?" she asked, holding it up for Leo to examine.

Leo took the drive, turning it over in his hands. "Let's find out."

Back in the familiar, cluttered sanctuary of Leo's office, the USB drive revealed its secrets. Encrypted messages between Dvorak and an unidentified individual discussing Adrian's project, financial records tracing to offshore accounts, and, most damningly, a recording of Dvorak admitting to orchestrating the sabotage.

"This is it," Maggie breathed, a tremor of excitement and relief in her voice. "This is undeniable proof of Dvorak's involvement."

"Involvement, yes," Leo corrected, his expression still grave. "But not necessarily *sole* guilt. The chain of responsibility might extend further."

Maggie frowned. "You still think Novotny might be involved?"

"It's possible," Leo admitted. "Capricorns are strategic, efficient. Using intermediaries is a common tactic." He considered the complex interplay of personalities, the Leo's need for control, the Capricorn's calculated planning.

The weight of the case, the constant tension, began to take its toll. As the night wore on, Leo became increasingly withdrawn, his usual intensity replaced by a haunted silence. Maggie sensed the shift, waiting patiently until they were alone.

"This is affecting you deeply, isn't it?" she said softly. "Bringing back memories of your sister."

Leo stiffened, momentarily surprised by her insight. He turned away, his gaze fixed on the city lights shimmering in the distance. "The betrayals... they resonate," he admitted, his voice raw with emotion. "A painful echo of my own failure to protect her."

Maggie gently placed a hand on his arm, a gesture of quiet support and understanding. "You're not failing now, Leo. We're in this together."

For a brief, vulnerable moment, Leo's defenses softened, revealing the raw pain beneath. "I just... I need to believe that justice is achievable. That it's not just an illusion."

"It's *not* an illusion," Maggie affirmed, her voice strong and unwavering. "And we *will* achieve it. For Adrian, for your sister, and for everyone who has been wronged. We'll find the complete truth, together." Her words were a vow, a shared commitment to a cause that transcended their personal struggles, a beacon of hope in the encroaching darkness.

Dvorak Technologies' headquarters was a modern monolith of glass and steel, a testament to its owner's success. Inside, a controlled energy thrummed, employees moving with purpose amidst the glow of screens displaying intricate code. But stepping into Alexander Dvorak's corner office was like entering a different world – a realm of calculated calm, of power subtly displayed. Floor-to-ceiling windows offered a panoramic view of Prague, a fitting backdrop for a man who seemed to see himself as a master of his domain. The room was designed to intimidate, to impress, to project an image of unshakeable control. *Leo territory*, Leo thought, taking in the opulent, yet carefully curated, surroundings.

Dvorak rose from his expansive leather chair as they entered, his smile smooth and practiced, but his eyes betraying a flicker of assessment. He exuded a charismatic authority, but Leo sensed a tension beneath the surface, a carefully guarded unease.

"Detective Maxwell," Dvorak said, his voice a polished baritone, extending a hand. "And Ms. Hart. What brings you to my office?"

Leo bypassed the offered handshake, placing the USB drive directly on the pristine surface of Dvorak's desk. "We recovered this from Adrian Varga's apartment. Perhaps you could explain its contents."

Dvorak's smile wavered, a brief, almost imperceptible crack in his façade before he regained his composure. "I'm afraid I don't recognize it."

Maggie leaned forward, her voice sharp and direct, cutting through the pleasantries. "It contains encrypted communications between you and an unidentified individual, discussing Adrian's project. Financial records linking to offshore accounts. And a recording – your own voice, Mr. Dvorak – admitting to orchestrating the sabotage."

A muscle in Dvorak's jaw tightened, a subtle but telling reaction. His tone, however, remained even. "Even assuming that's authentic, it doesn't prove I was responsible for his death."

"No," Leo agreed, his voice low and steady. "But it establishes a clear motive – and the means to carry out the plan." He watched Dvorak closely, searching for any crack in his Leo persona.

Dvorak hesitated, then let out a carefully calibrated sigh, a performance of weary frustration. "Look, Adrian and I had our disagreements, certainly. But I would never resort to violence. He was... a talented individual. Perhaps misguided, but talented."

Leo and Maggie exchanged a quick, knowing glance. Dvorak wasn't denying his involvement; he was attempting to reframe it, to deflect responsibility. The classic Leo tactic – control the narrative, maintain the image.

Before they could press him further, Dvorak stood abruptly, effectively terminating the meeting. "If you'll excuse me, I have another pressing engagement. My assistant will see you out."

Outside the office, Maggie turned to Leo, her voice a mix of frustration and determination. "He's concealing something, Leo. It's obvious."

"Agreed," Leo replied, his expression grim. "But without more concrete evidence, we can't prove anything definitive. We need to intensify our focus on his connection to Novotny – and unravel the truth about 'Balance Keeper.'" He was already thinking about their next move, about how to penetrate Dvorak's carefully constructed defenses. The Lion's den was proving to be a challenging, and dangerous, place.

THE WEIGHT OF THEIR discoveries pressed down on Leo and Maggie as they met in a quiet café, the morning bustle of Wenceslas Square a distant, muted hum. Steam curled from their coffee cups, a fragile counterpoint to the complex web of deceit they were untangling. They needed to connect Dvorak's actions back to Novotny, to find the definitive link.

"We know Dvorak orchestrated the sabotage," Maggie began, her voice low and intense, tapping a pen against her notebook. "But he wouldn't act in isolation. Someone else was involved – either directing him or providing cover."

Leo nodded, his gaze distant, his mind already sifting through the possibilities, filtering them through his understanding of behavioral patterns. *Novotny. Capricorn.* The pragmatic, calculating strategist, the master of long-term planning... the one who eliminated obstacles with ruthless efficiency. "If Novotny perceived Adrian's project as a threat, he wouldn't hesitate to act. But he'd do it indirectly, through intermediaries."

"Novotny fits that profile perfectly," Leo agreed, his voice a thoughtful murmur. "He possesses the discipline to avoid impulsive actions, but also the ruthlessness to orchestrate events from the shadows, maintaining a safe distance."

"But why involve Dvorak?" Maggie questioned, her brow furrowed. "Why not handle the situation directly?"

"Because a Capricorn, especially someone like Novotny, prioritizes efficiency and self-preservation," Leo explained. "Using intermediaries creates a buffer. Plausible deniability. He can distance himself from any negative repercussions." He pictured Novotny, a meticulous planner, carefully positioning others to take the risks.

Maggie frowned, her mind racing, connecting the dots. "So, what's our next step? Do we confront Novotny again, armed with this new information?"

"No," Leo replied decisively. "Not yet. We need more than circumstantial evidence. We need irrefutable proof linking him to Dvorak's actions. Our immediate focus should be Novotny Solutions – we need to uncover any and all connections to 'Balance Keeper.'" He was already formulating a plan, a strategy to penetrate Novotny's defenses.

The sterile, almost oppressive atmosphere of Novotny Solutions greeted them later that afternoon. They returned under the guise of auditors, conducting a routine review of the company's cybersecurity protocols. Maggie, leveraging her journalistic credentials, had requested access to financial records, while Leo, posing as a consultant, focused on client lists – a carefully constructed deception facilitated by Maggie's network.

Inside the sleek, modern building, employees moved with a quiet, almost unsettling precision, their attention seemingly glued to the screens before them. The space felt less like a collaborative environment and more like a carefully guarded fortress, designed to protect secrets at all costs.

When they were finally ushered into Novotny's office, the man himself greeted them with a polished smile that failed to mask the underlying calculation in his eyes. *The Capricorn mask*, Leo thought, observing Novotny's controlled demeanor, his carefully chosen words.

"Ms. Hart," Novotny said, his voice smooth and controlled, extending a hand. "And Mr. Maxwell. What brings you back to Novotny Solutions?"

"We're conducting a review of current cybersecurity practices," Maggie replied, maintaining a neutral, professional tone. "Your firm has certainly established a strong reputation."

Novotny nodded, his expression carefully guarded, revealing nothing. "Innovation is our core value. But I suspect your interest extends beyond mere industry observation."

Leo stepped forward, his gaze unwavering. "We're also interested in exploring potential collaborations – specifically, between Novotny Solutions and Dvorak Technologies. Any information you could provide would be greatly appreciated."

The polished smile flickered, a subtle, almost imperceptible shift in Novotny's composure. He quickly regained his control. "Dvorak and I have collaborated on various projects over the years. Standard industry procedure."

"Including any projects related to Adrian Varga?" Maggie interjected, her voice taking on a slightly sharper edge.

A muscle in Novotny's jaw tightened, a brief, involuntary betrayal of his inner state. "Adrian's work was certainly innovative, but ultimately unsustainable. I personally cautioned him about the potential risks."

Leo and Maggie exchanged a quick, knowing glance. They had touched a nerve, a vulnerability in Novotny's carefully constructed façade.

Before they could press further, Novotny abruptly stood, effectively terminating the meeting. "If you'll excuse me, a prior engagement requires my attention. My assistant will see you out."

Outside Novotny's office, Maggie turned to Leo, her voice low and urgent. "He's definitely hiding something."

"Agreed," Leo said grimly. "But we still lack concrete evidence. We need to intensify our focus on their collaboration – and find the definitive link to 'Balance Keeper.'"

Back in the familiar clutter of Leo's office that evening, they immersed themselves in the documents Maggie had obtained through her network. Among them, a series of emails detailing a joint venture between Novotny Solutions and Dvorak Technologies – the project codenamed "Balance Keeper."

"This could be the breakthrough," Maggie murmured, her voice filled with a mix of excitement and apprehension. "If we can definitively link this project to Adrian's murder, we'll have the proof we need."

"But how do we establish that connection?" Leo countered, his voice laced with frustration. "Without direct evidence, it remains circumstantial, easily dismissed."

Maggie paused, considering their options. "We could try another confrontation with Novotny," she suggested hesitantly. "Present him with this information. See if he makes a mistake."

Leo shook his head firmly. "That's too dangerous. He's already demonstrated a willingness to eliminate perceived threats. We need a different approach. Something less direct." He tapped a finger on the corkboard, his mind already formulating a new strategy.

Before they could refine their plan, Leo's phone vibrated. Another anonymous text: "The scales tip soon. Choose wisely."

Maggie read the message over his shoulder, a knot of worry tightening in her chest. "What does that even mean?"

"It means our time is limited," Leo replied, his voice heavy with a sense of impending urgency. "Whoever is sending these messages is preparing to act – and we're caught in the middle."

The weight of the case, the constant pressure, began to take its toll. As the hours passed, Leo became increasingly withdrawn, his usual intensity replaced by a quiet introspection. Maggie sensed the shift, and when they were finally alone, she spoke softly, her voice filled with concern.

"This is bringing back painful memories, isn't it?" she asked gently. "Memories of your sister."

Leo stiffened, momentarily surprised by her insight. He turned away, his gaze fixed on the city lights shimmering in the distance. "Cases like this... where trust is so completely violated... it's difficult not to think of her," he admitted, his voice raw with emotion. "Of my own inability to prevent what happened."

Maggie gently placed a hand on his arm, a gesture of quiet support and understanding. "You're doing everything you can now, Leo. For Adrian, for Lukáš, for the very principle of justice. Don't let the past consume you."

For a brief moment, Leo's defenses wavered, revealing the raw, enduring pain beneath. "I just... I don't want to fail again."

"And you won't," Maggie said, her voice filled with a quiet strength. "Not while we're working together. We'll find the truth. We have to." Her words were a pledge, a shared commitment to a cause that transcended their personal struggles, a fragile alliance forged in the pursuit of justice.

Returning to the digital realm, Leo and Maggie meticulously re-examined Adrian's encrypted files, their focus narrowed on finding any overlooked connections between

Novotny Solutions and "Balance Keeper." The data was a dense thicket of information, but Maggie, with a sudden sharp intake of breath, unearthed something significant.

"These emails," she said, her voice edged with urgency, "they're between Adrian and someone using the alias 'Project Oversight.' And the dates... they're from just days before he died."

Leo leaned closer, his eyes quickly absorbing the content. The emails contained a heated exchange – Adrian accusing the anonymous sender of misusing confidential Project Phoenix information.

A muscle in Leo's jaw tightened. The careful orchestration, the manipulation... it all felt chillingly familiar. *Novotny.* He could almost picture the man, a meticulous planner, operating from the shadows. "If Adrian threatened to expose him, to disrupt his control..." he murmured, the implication hanging heavy in the air.

"But why such an elaborate scheme?" Maggie wondered, her brow furrowed in thought. "Why not just shut down the project directly?"

"Because a Capricorn, especially someone like Novotny, doesn't just react; he strategizes," Leo explained, his voice reflecting a grudging admiration for his adversary's cunning. "It's not solely about silencing Adrian; it's about controlling the narrative. About sending a message." He pictured Novotny, not as a brute force, but as a chess master, meticulously planning each move.

Their analysis was interrupted by the insistent vibration of Maggie's phone. Another anonymous text: "The truth is closer than you think. Look to the stars."

Maggie showed Leo the message, her expression a mixture of frustration and bewilderment. "Another Zodiac riddle? What is this, some kind of twisted game?"

"Perhaps," Leo mused, his fingers tapping a thoughtful rhythm on the table. "Or perhaps someone is attempting to guide us, using the Zodiac as a... code. A cryptic set of instructions."

"Or maybe it *is* a genuine offer of help," Maggie suggested, a flicker of hope in her voice. "Could 'look to the stars' be literal? Referring to someone's astrological sign?"

Leo's gaze sharpened. Novotny, the calculated Capricorn, was an obvious suspect, but a persistent, nagging doubt remained. "Is it possible there's another player we've overlooked? Someone operating just beyond our perception?"

Seeking clarification on the "Project Oversight" alias, they decided to revisit Lukáš Horák that afternoon. At his safehouse, Lukáš greeted them with a visible tremor, his hands shaking as he held a cup of tea. The picture of a Virgo under pressure.

"You've discovered something," he stated, his voice a low, nervous murmur, his eyes darting between them.

"We have," Maggie confirmed, showing him the printed emails. "Do you recognize this account?"

Lukáš hesitated, then nodded slowly. "It... it's the same alias I used. For the leak. But I swear, I stopped after Adrian confronted me."

Leo studied him intently, observing his behavior, looking for the subtle cues that might reveal more than his words. *Virgo.* Detail-oriented, adaptable, but also prone to anxiety and guilt when under pressure. "Did anyone else have access to your account?"

"No," Lukáš insisted, then paused, his voice dropping to a near whisper. "But... someone *knew* about it. Someone approached me... after Adrian died."

"Who?" Maggie pressed, her voice sharp and insistent.

Lukáš swallowed hard. "Novotny. He said... he could offer me protection. If I cooperated."

A look of grim understanding passed between Leo and Maggie. The puzzle pieces were falling into place, forming a disturbing image.

"Novotny's playing a complex game," Leo stated, his voice hard. "Using Lukáš as a pawn, while simultaneously diverting suspicion from himself, and Dvorak."

"But why Lukáš?" Maggie asked.

"Efficiency and deniability. Classic Capricorn"

The weight of their discoveries pressed upon them as they left Lukáš's safehouse. "We need concrete evidence, Leo," Maggie said, her voice filled with urgency. "Something that definitively links Novotny to Adrian's murder."

"I know," Leo replied, his gaze distant, his mind already formulating a plan. "And I have an idea where we might find it."

A sense of foreboding hung in the air as they returned to Adrian's apartment that evening, the scene of the crime. Despite previous forensic examinations, Leo felt a persistent intuition, a belief that a crucial piece of evidence remained, waiting to be discovered.

"Capricorns, for all their meticulous planning, might leave a subtle trace," Leo murmured, his eyes scanning the room with careful attention. "A behavioral signature, a reflection of their need for control."

Maggie nodded, joining the search. They moved through the disarray, a synchronized effort born of shared purpose. It was Maggie who spotted it – a faint glint of metal beneath the sofa, partially obscured by dust. A small USB drive.

"What's this?" she asked, holding it up for Leo to examine.

Leo took the drive, turning it over in his hands. "Let's find out."

Back in the familiar, cluttered sanctuary of Leo's office, the USB drive yielded its secrets. Encrypted messages between Novotny and an unidentified individual discussing Adrian's project, financial records tracing to offshore accounts, and, most damningly, a recording of Novotny admitting to orchestrating the sabotage.

"This is it," Maggie breathed, a tremor of excitement and relief in her voice. "This is undeniable proof of Novotny's involvement."

"Involvement, yes," Leo corrected, his expression still grave. "But not necessarily *sole* guilt. The chain of command could extend further."

Maggie frowned. "You still think Dvorak might be involved?"

"It's more than possible," Leo admitted. "Leos crave dominance, and would happily use a Capricorn's meticulous nature" He considered the complex interplay of personalities, the Leo's need for control, the Capricorn's calculated planning. And how well they can work together.

JUSTICE IN THE SHADOWS

The weight of the case, and the past, settled heavily on Leo as the night wore on. Maggie, sensing his shift in mood, waited patiently until they were alone.

"This is stirring up a lot for you, isn't it?" she said softly. "Bringing back memories of your sister."

Leo stiffened, momentarily surprised by her insight. He turned away, his gaze fixed on the city lights spread out before them. "Cases like this... where trust is so thoroughly betrayed... it's hard not to think of her," he admitted, his voice rough with emotion. "Of my own failure to protect her."

Maggie gently placed a hand on his arm, a gesture of quiet support. "You're not failing now, Leo. We're a team."

For a fleeting moment, Leo's defenses crumbled, revealing the raw pain beneath. "I just... I need to believe that justice is possible. That we can make a difference."

"It *is* possible," Maggie affirmed, her voice strong and unwavering. "And we *will* make a difference. For Adrian, for your sister, and for everyone who has been wronged. We'll uncover the complete truth, together." Her words were a vow, a shared commitment to a cause that transcended their personal pain, a source of strength in the face of overwhelming darkness.

one thing—we're closer to the truth than we've ever been. And that means something."

Leo nodded slowly, his jaw unclenching as he finally allowed himself to believe her. Armed with the USB drive and a sharpened resolve, Leo and Maggie returned to Novotny Solutions. The sleek, modern building hummed with activity, but a sense of unease settled over them as they approached Novotny's office. This time, there would be no pretense, no carefully crafted facade.

Novotny greeted them with his usual polished smile, but it didn't reach his eyes, betraying a flicker of apprehension. *The Capricorn, ever vigilant*, Leo thought, noting the man's controlled demeanor.

"Back so soon?" Novotny inquired smoothly, gesturing for them to sit. "Have you, perhaps, reconsidered my innocence?"

Leo ignored the veiled sarcasm, placing the USB drive squarely on Novotny's pristine desk. "We recovered this from Adrian's apartment. Perhaps you'd care to explain its contents."

The smile faltered, a brief, almost imperceptible crack in Novotny's composure. His voice, however, remained steady. "I have no idea what that is. I've never seen it before."

Maggie leaned forward, her voice sharp, cutting through the pleasantries. "It contains encrypted communications between you and an unidentified individual, discussing Adrian's project. Financial records linking to offshore accounts. And a recording – your own voice, Mr. Novotny – admitting to orchestrating the sabotage."

A muscle in Novotny's jaw twitched, a subtle but telling sign of his internal struggle. He recovered quickly. "Even if that were authentic, it doesn't prove I was responsible for his death."

"No," Leo agreed, his voice low and controlled. "But it establishes a clear motive – and the means to carry out the plan." He watched Novotny closely, searching for any further cracks in his Capricorn façade.

Novotny hesitated, then let out a weary sigh, a calculated display of resignation. "Alright. I admit I wasn't entirely truthful before. Adrian's project posed a significant threat to my company's interests. But I would *never* harm him."

"Yet someone *did*," Maggie countered, her voice unwavering. "And whoever it was left a trail of clues leading directly to you."

Novotny's expression shifted, a flicker of anger replacing the carefully constructed mask of composure. "If you're accusing me of murder, you'd better have concrete proof."

"We're getting closer," Leo replied, his voice a low, steady threat. "And when we do, you'll wish you'd been more forthcoming from the beginning."

As they continued to press Novotny, Leo observed subtle shifts in his behavior – the tightened jaw, the slightly more rapid breathing, the carefully chosen words. *The Capricorn under pressure*, he thought, noting how the man's calm exterior was beginning to crumble, revealing glimpses of the ruthless pragmatism beneath.

"You think you understand what's at stake here?" Novotny snapped, his voice rising slightly, a crack in his controlled demeanor. "You have no idea. Adrian was meddling with forces he didn't comprehend. If he hadn't pushed so hard, none of this would have happened."

"What forces?" Maggie pressed, her voice sharp and insistent.

Novotny hesitated, then shook his head. "I'm not saying anything further without legal counsel."

Leo and Maggie exchanged a quick, knowing glance. They had reached an impasse, but not before uncovering a significant revelation. Novotny's carefully constructed defenses had momentarily crumbled, revealing a glimpse of something darker, something more complex.

Later that evening, back in the familiar, cluttered sanctuary of Leo's office, they reviewed the evidence, piecing together the timeline of events, analyzing Novotny's reactions.

"So, Novotny admits to orchestrating the sabotage," Maggie mused, tapping a pen against her notebook. "But why such an extreme measure? Why not simply discredit the project, undermine it quietly?"

"Because a Capricorn, when threatened, doesn't just react; they control," Leo explained, his voice reflecting a grim understanding. "Killing Adrian wasn't just about silencing him; it was about sending a message. A warning to anyone else who might consider crossing him."

"But who was ultimately pulling the strings?" Maggie pressed. "Novotny is too calculating to act alone, unless..."

"Unless he believed he *was* acting independently," Leo finished, his voice heavy with a sense of dawning realization. "A Leo, like Dvorak, craves dominance and control – and would readily exploit a Capricorn's meticulous nature." He considered the complex interplay of personalities, the web of deceit and manipulation.

Maggie nodded slowly, then paused, a thoughtful expression on her face. "What about Evan? Do you think he's still concealing something?"

"It's certainly possible," Leo admitted. "Scorpios are secretive by nature – and also prone to vengeance. If Evan felt betrayed by Adrian, it could have clouded his judgment, made him susceptible to manipulation."

The weight of the case, the constant pressure, began to take its toll. As the hours passed, Leo became increasingly withdrawn, his usual intensity replaced by a quiet introspection. Maggie, sensing his shift in mood, waited patiently until they were alone.

"This is bringing up a lot for you, isn't it?" she asked softly, her voice filled with concern. "Memories of your sister."

Leo stiffened, momentarily surprised by her insight. He turned away, his gaze fixed on the city lights spread out before them. He said nothing.

Maggie got closer.

"I don't pretend to understand all that you have pass, all that you feel".

Chapter 10

The aroma of strong coffee filled the air as Leo and Maggie met at their usual café, the morning light filtering through the windows, illuminating the serious expressions on their faces. They needed to dissect the evidence, to trace the connection between Novotny and Dvorak, and to uncover the full extent of their involvement in Adrian's murder.

"Novotny admitted to orchestrating the sabotage," Maggie began, her voice low and thoughtful, tapping a pen against her notebook. "But he wouldn't have acted alone. Someone else was either directing him – or providing cover."

Leo nodded, his gaze distant, his mind already constructing a behavioral profile of Dvorak. *Leo.* The inherent pride, the ambition, the need for control... it all pointed to a capacity for ruthless manipulation, for orchestrating events from afar. "If Dvorak perceived Adrian's project as a threat to his own power, his carefully constructed empire, he wouldn't hesitate to act. But he'd do it indirectly, through intermediaries."

"Dvorak certainly fits that profile," Leo agreed, his voice a thoughtful murmur. "He possesses the ego to demand absolute obedience, but also the calculated detachment to avoid any direct implication. He wouldn't get his hands dirty, but he'd pull the strings from the shadows."

"But why use Novotny?" Maggie questioned, her brow furrowed in thought. "Why not eliminate the threat himself?"

"Because a Leo, especially someone in Dvorak's position, is acutely aware of appearances," Leo explained. "Using an intermediary provides a layer of protection. Plausible deniability. He can distance himself from any negative consequences, maintaining his carefully crafted image." He pictured Dvorak, a master manipulator, positioning Novotny as a pawn in his game.

Maggie frowned, her mind racing, connecting the dots. "So, what's our next step? Do we confront Dvorak again, armed with what we know about Novotny?"

"No," Leo replied decisively. "Not yet. We need more than circumstantial evidence. We need irrefutable proof linking him to Novotny's actions, to the murder itself. Our immediate focus should be Dvorak Technologies – we need to uncover any and all connections to 'Balance Keeper.'"

The imposing, sterile atmosphere of Dvorak Technologies greeted them later that afternoon. They returned under the guise of auditors, conducting a routine review of the company's cybersecurity protocols. Maggie, leveraging her journalistic credentials, had requested access to financial records, while Leo, posing as a consultant, focused on client lists – a carefully orchestrated deception facilitated by Maggie's network.

Inside the sleek, modern building, employees moved with a quiet, almost unsettling precision, their attention seemingly glued to the screens before them. The space felt less like a collaborative environment and more like a carefully guarded fortress.

When they were finally ushered into Dvorak's office, the man himself greeted them with a polished smile that failed to mask the underlying assessment in his eyes. *The Lion, sizing up his prey*, Leo observed, noting Dvorak's controlled demeanor, the subtle cues of a Leo's calculated charm.

"Ms. Hart," Dvorak said, his voice a smooth baritone, extending a hand. "And Mr. Maxwell. What brings you back to Dvorak Technologies?"

"We're conducting a review of current cybersecurity practices," Maggie replied, maintaining a neutral, professional tone. "Your firm has certainly established a strong reputation."

Dvorak acknowledged the compliment with a slight nod, a flicker of something unreadable in his eyes. "Innovation is our core value. But I suspect your interest extends beyond mere industry observation."

Leo stepped forward, his gaze unwavering. "We're also interested in exploring potential collaborations – specifically, between Dvorak Technologies and Novotny Solutions. Any insights you might share would be invaluable."

The polished smile wavered, a subtle shift in Dvorak's composure. He quickly regained his control. "Novotny and I have partnered on various ventures over the years. Standard industry procedure."

"Including any related to Adrian Varga?" Maggie interjected, her voice taking on a slightly sharper edge.

A muscle in Dvorak's jaw tightened, a brief, involuntary betrayal of his inner state. "Adrian's work was undeniably groundbreaking, but ultimately flawed. I personally cautioned him about the inherent risks."

Leo and Maggie exchanged a quick, knowing glance. They had touched a nerve, a vulnerability in Dvorak's carefully constructed façade.

Before they could press further, Dvorak abruptly stood, effectively terminating the meeting. "If you'll excuse me, a prior engagement requires my attention. My assistant will escort you out."

Outside Dvorak's office, Maggie turned to Leo, her voice low and urgent. "He's definitely hiding something."

"Without question," Leo agreed, his expression grim. "But we still lack concrete evidence. We need to dig deeper into their collaboration – and expose the truth about 'Balance Keeper.'"

Later, in the familiar clutter of Leo's office, they immersed themselves in the documents Maggie had acquired. Among them, a series of emails detailed a joint venture between Dvorak Technologies and Novotny Solutions – the project codenamed "Balance Keeper."

"This could be the key," Maggie whispered, her voice filled with a mix of excitement and apprehension. "If we can definitively link this project to Adrian's murder, we'll have the proof we need."

"But how do we establish that link?" Leo countered, his voice laced with frustration. "Without direct evidence, it's all circumstantial, easily refuted."

Maggie paused, considering their options. "Perhaps it's time for a calculated gamble. We confront Dvorak – present him with this information. Force him to react, to reveal something."

Leo shook his head firmly. "That's too risky. He's already demonstrated a willingness to eliminate perceived threats. We need a different strategy. Something that targets his Leo vulnerabilities – his pride, his need for control." He began to pace, his mind formulating a new plan.

Before they could solidify their next move, Leo's phone vibrated. Another anonymous text: "The scales tip soon. Choose wisely."

Maggie read the message over his shoulder, a knot of worry tightening in her chest. "What does that even mean?"

"It means our window of opportunity is closing," Leo replied, his voice heavy with a sense of impending urgency. "Whoever is sending these messages is about to make a move – and we're caught in the middle."

The weight of the case, the constant pressure, began to take its toll. As the night wore on, Leo became increasingly introspective, his usual intensity replaced by a quiet contemplation. Maggie sensed the shift, and when they were finally alone, she spoke softly, her voice filled with concern.

"This case... it's stirring up a lot for you, isn't it?" she asked gently. "Bringing back memories of your sister."

Leo stiffened slightly, momentarily surprised by her insight. He turned away, his gaze fixed on the cityscape spread out before them. "Cases like this... where trust is so thoroughly betrayed... it's hard not to think of her," he admitted, his voice tinged with a raw, enduring pain. "Of my own inability to help her."

Maggie gently placed a hand on his arm, a gesture of quiet support and understanding. "You're doing everything you can

JUSTICE IN THE SHADOWS 111

now, Leo. For Adrian, for Lukáš, for justice itself. Don't let the past paralyze you."

For a brief moment, Leo's defenses wavered, revealing the vulnerability beneath. "I just... I don't want to fail again, Maggie."

"You won't," Maggie said, her voice filled with a quiet strength. "Not while we're working together. We'll find the truth. We have to." Her words were a promise, a shared commitment to a cause that transcended their personal struggles, a fragile alliance forged in the pursuit of justice, and the fight against the manipulative forces arrayed against them.

Returning to their investigation, Leo and Maggie delved back into Adrian's encrypted files, searching for any previously missed connections between Dvorak Technologies and "Balance Keeper." The digital archive was a dense tangle of information, but Maggie, with a sudden sharp intake of breath, unearthed a crucial detail.

"These emails," she said, her voice tight with urgency, "they're between Adrian and someone using the alias 'Project Oversight.' And look at the dates – they're from just days before he was killed."

Leo leaned closer, his eyes quickly scanning the content. The emails revealed a heated exchange – Adrian accusing the anonymous sender of misusing confidential Project Phoenix information.

A muscle in Leo's jaw tightened. The meticulous orchestration, the calculated manipulation... it all pointed to Dvorak's influence. *Leo.* The need for dominance, the willingness to eliminate any perceived threat... "If Adrian threatened his position, his control..." he murmured, the implication hanging heavy in the air.

"But why such an indirect, convoluted approach?" Maggie wondered, her brow furrowed in thought. "Why not simply shut down the project?"

"Because a Leo, especially someone like Dvorak, doesn't just react; he *performs*," Leo explained, his voice reflecting a grim understanding of his adversary's mindset. "It's not solely about silencing Adrian; it's about demonstrating power, about controlling the narrative." He pictured Dvorak, a master manipulator, enjoying the unfolding chaos from a safe distance.

Their analysis was interrupted by the insistent vibration of Maggie's phone. Another anonymous text: "The truth is closer than you think. Look to the stars."

Maggie showed Leo the message, her expression a mix of frustration and bewilderment. "Another cryptic Zodiac message? Is this a game to whoever is sending these?"

"Perhaps," Leo mused, his fingers tapping a thoughtful rhythm on the table. "Or perhaps someone is attempting to guide us, using the Zodiac as a... language. A set of coded instructions."

"Or maybe it *is* genuine help," Maggie offered, a sliver of hope in her voice. "Could 'look to the stars' be a literal instruction? Referring to someone's astrological sign?"

Leo's gaze sharpened. Dvorak, the domineering Leo, was the primary suspect, but a persistent, nagging doubt remained. "Could there be another player involved? Someone operating just beyond our current understanding?"

Seeking clarification on the "Project Oversight" alias, they decided to revisit Lukáš Horák later that afternoon. At his safehouse, Lukáš greeted them with a visible tremor, his hands shaking as he held a cup of tea. The anxieties of a Virgo under pressure, Leo observed.

"You've discovered something," he stated, his voice a low, nervous murmur, his eyes darting between them.

"We have," Maggie confirmed, showing him the printed emails. "Do you recognize this account?"

Lukáš hesitated, then nodded slowly. "It... it's the same alias I used. When I leaked the data. But I swear, I stopped after Adrian confronted me."

Leo studied him intently, observing his behavior, looking for the subtle cues that might reveal more than his words. *Virgo*. Detail-oriented, adaptable, but also prone to anxiety and guilt when caught in a compromising situation. "Did anyone else have access to your account?"

"No," Lukáš insisted, then paused, his voice dropping to a near whisper. "But... someone *knew* about it. Someone approached me... after Adrian died."

"Who?" Maggie pressed, her voice sharp and insistent.

Lukáš swallowed hard. "Dvorak. He said... he could offer me protection. If I cooperated."

A look of grim understanding passed between Leo and Maggie. The puzzle pieces were falling into place, creating a disturbing image.

"Dvorak's playing a complex game," Leo stated, his voice hard. "Using Lukáš as a pawn, while simultaneously maintaining his own distance from the crime."

"But why involve, Lukáš, and let him take the blame?" Maggie questioned.

"Control." Leo said.

The need for undeniable evidence weighed heavily on them as they left Lukáš's safehouse. "We need something concrete, Leo," Maggie said, her voice filled with urgency. "Something that directly and irrefutably links Dvorak to Adrian's murder."

"I know," Leo replied, his gaze distant, his mind already formulating a plan. "And I have a feeling where we might find it."

A palpable sense of unease settled over them as they returned to Adrian's apartment that evening, the scene of the crime. Despite previous forensic examinations, Leo felt a persistent intuition, a belief that a crucial piece of evidence remained hidden, overlooked by everyone else.

"A Leo, even in orchestrating a crime, might leave a subtle trace," Leo murmured, his eyes scanning the room with meticulous care. "A touch of ego, a behavioral signature, something reflecting his need for control." He wasn't looking for obvious clues, but for something that resonated with Dvorak's personality.

Maggie nodded, joining the search. They moved through the disarray, a synchronized effort born of shared purpose and determination. It was Maggie who spotted it – a faint glint of metal beneath the sofa, partially hidden by a layer of dust. A small, almost insignificant-looking USB drive.

"What's this?" she asked, holding it up for Leo to examine.

Leo took the drive, turning it over in his hands. "Let's find out."

Back in the familiar, cluttered sanctuary of Leo's office, the USB drive revealed its secrets. Encrypted messages between Dvorak and an unidentified individual discussing Adrian's project, financial records tracing to offshore accounts, and, most damningly, a recording of Dvorak admitting to orchestrating the sabotage.

"This is it," Maggie breathed, a tremor of excitement and relief in her voice. "This is undeniable proof of Dvorak's direct involvement."

"Involvement, yes," Leo corrected, his expression still grave. "But not necessarily *sole* responsibility. The chain of command could still extend further. Novotny may still be involved."

Maggie frowned. "You really think so?"

"Capricorns are efficient and pragmatic, it would be like him," Leo replied, he thought about their behaviors, and this made more sense.

The weight of the case, pressing down on them.

Maggie adress Leo

"We are not just looking for an answer, we are seeking justice for those who can not" Maggie said

Leo, surprised, turn to her.

THE STERILE ELEGANCE of Dvorak Technologies felt more like a stage than an office as Leo and Maggie returned, armed with the damning evidence from the USB drive. Their determination was a palpable force, a counterpoint to the carefully controlled environment. They were ready to confront the Lion in his den.

Dvorak greeted them with his usual practiced smile, but this time, Leo detected a flicker of unease behind the Leo's mask of confidence. The man was clearly in control of his space, but the air held a subtle tension.

"Back so soon?" Dvorak inquired smoothly, gesturing for them to sit. "Have you, perhaps, reconsidered my lack of involvement?"

Leo ignored the feigned innocence, placing the USB drive squarely on Dvorak's immaculate desk. "We recovered this from Adrian's apartment. I believe you're familiar with its contents."

Dvorak's smile wavered, a fleeting crack in his otherwise impeccable composure. His voice, however, remained steady. "I've no idea what that is."

Maggie leaned forward, her voice sharp, cutting through the pretense. "It contains encrypted communications between you and an unidentified individual, discussing Adrian's project. Financial records linking to offshore accounts. And a recording – your own voice, Mr. Dvorak – admitting to orchestrating the sabotage."

A muscle in Dvorak's jaw tightened, a subtle but telling betrayal of his internal struggle. He recovered swiftly. "Even if that were authentic – and I'm not admitting that it is – it doesn't prove I was responsible for his death."

"No," Leo agreed, his voice low and controlled. "But it establishes a clear motive – and the means to carry out the plan." He watched Dvorak intently, searching for any further sign of weakness, any crack in his Leo's carefully constructed façade.

Dvorak hesitated, then let out a calculated sigh, a performance of weary resignation. "Alright. I admit I wasn't entirely forthright. Adrian's project posed a significant threat to my interests. But I would *never* resort to murder."

"Yet someone *did*," Maggie countered, her voice unwavering. "And the evidence points directly to you."

Dvorak's expression shifted, a flicker of anger replacing the mask of composure. "If you're accusing me of murder, you'd better have irrefutable proof."

"We're getting closer," Leo replied, his voice a low, steady threat. "And when we do, you'll wish you'd cooperated from the beginning."

As they continued to press Dvorak, Leo observed subtle shifts in his behavior – the tightened jaw, the slightly accelerated breathing, the carefully chosen words. *The Leo under pressure*, he thought, noting how the man's outward confidence was beginning to fray, revealing glimpses of the ruthless determination beneath.

"You think you understand what's at stake here?" Dvorak snapped, his voice rising slightly, a crack in his controlled demeanor. "You have no *idea*. Adrian was meddling with forces he didn't comprehend. If he hadn't pushed so hard, none of this would have happened."

"What forces?" Maggie pressed, her voice sharp and insistent.

Dvorak hesitated, then shook his head, his eyes hardening. "I'm not saying anything further without legal counsel."

Leo and Maggie exchanged a quick, knowing glance. They had reached an impasse, but not before uncovering a significant revelation. Dvorak's carefully constructed defenses had momentarily crumbled, revealing a glimpse of something darker, something more complex than they had initially anticipated.

Later, back in the relative chaos of Leo's office, amidst the corkboard and scattered files, they re-examined the evidence, piecing together the timeline, analyzing Dvorak's reactions.

"So, Dvorak admits to orchestrating the sabotage," Maggie mused, tapping a pen against her notebook. "But he's still holding something back. Why go to such extremes? Why not simply discredit the project, undermine it quietly?"

"Because a Leo, driven by ego and a need for control, doesn't just neutralize a threat; he makes an *example* of them," Leo explained, his voice reflecting a grim understanding. "Killing Adrian wasn't just about silencing him; it was about sending a message. A warning to anyone else who dared to challenge him."

"But who was ultimately in charge?" Maggie pressed. "Dvorak's too proud to be a mere pawn. Unless..."

"Unless he believed he *was* in control," Leo finished, his voice heavy with a sense of dawning realization. "A Capricorn, like Novotny, would understand that. He could manipulate Dvorak's ego, use his need for dominance to his own advantage." He considered the complex interplay of personalities, the web of deceit and manipulation.

Maggie nodded slowly, then paused, a thoughtful expression on her face. "What about Evan? Do you think he's still withholding information?"

"It's certainly possible," Leo admitted. "Scorpios are secretive by nature – and also capable of intense loyalty and vengeance. If Evan felt betrayed by Adrian, or by anyone else involved, it could have influenced his actions, made him a willing participant."

The weight of the unresolved questions, the constant pressure, pressed down on them.

Maggie decided to wait, to talk.

"You are not alone on this" she finally said.

Leo, turn his head.

Chapter 11

The familiar comfort of their usual café offered a brief respite from the mounting pressure of the case. As Leo and Maggie settled into their routine, the aroma of coffee filling the air, they revisited the evidence, seeking the crucial link between Dvorak's actions and Novotny's potential involvement.

"We know Dvorak orchestrated the sabotage," Maggie began, her voice low and thoughtful, stirring her coffee. "But he wouldn't have acted in isolation. Someone else was either directing him, providing cover, or... manipulating him."

Leo nodded, his gaze distant, his mind already analyzing the behavioral patterns, the interplay of personalities. *Novotny. Capricorn.* The meticulous planner, the strategist, the one who eliminated obstacles with cold efficiency. "If Novotny perceived Adrian's project as a threat, a challenge to his own operations, he wouldn't hesitate to act. But he'd do it indirectly, through someone like Dvorak."

"Novotny certainly fits the *profile* of someone who would orchestrate this," Leo agreed, his voice a thoughtful murmur. "He has the discipline to avoid impulsive actions, the ruthlessness to eliminate anyone in his path, and the strategic mind to do it all from the shadows."

"But why use Dvorak?" Maggie questioned, her brow furrowed in thought. "Why not handle it himself?"

"Because a Capricorn, especially someone like Novotny, values efficiency and self-preservation above all else," Leo explained. "Using an intermediary – especially someone with Dvorak's Leo ego – creates a buffer. Plausible deniability. He can distance himself from any negative consequences, maintaining his carefully constructed image of control."

Maggie frowned, her mind racing, connecting the dots. "So, what's our next move? Do we confront Novotny again, armed with the evidence implicating Dvorak?"

"No," Leo replied decisively. "Not yet. We need more than circumstantial evidence. We need *proof* that connects him directly to Dvorak's actions. Our immediate focus should be Novotny Solutions – we need to delve deeper into their operations, uncover any connection to 'Balance Keeper,' and expose the full extent of their collaboration with Dvorak."

Their strategy led them back to the sterile, almost intimidating environment of Novotny Solutions later that afternoon. They returned under the guise of auditors, conducting a routine review of the company's cybersecurity protocols. Maggie, leveraging her journalistic connections, had arranged access to financial records, while Leo, posing as a consultant, focused on client lists – a carefully planned deception designed to uncover hidden connections.

Inside the sleek, modern building, employees moved with a quiet, almost unsettling precision, their attention seemingly glued to the screens before them. The space felt less like a collaborative environment and more like a carefully guarded fortress, designed to protect secrets at all costs.

When they were finally ushered into Novotny's office, the man himself greeted them with a polished smile that failed to mask the underlying calculation in his eyes. *The Capricorn*, ever vigilant, Leo thought, observing Novotny's controlled demeanor.

"Ms. Hart," Novotny said, his voice smooth and controlled, extending a hand. "And Mr. Maxwell. What brings you back to Novotny Solutions?"

"We're conducting a review of current cybersecurity practices," Maggie replied, maintaining a neutral, professional tone. "Your firm has certainly established a strong reputation."

Novotny nodded, his expression carefully guarded, revealing nothing. "Innovation is our core value. But I suspect your interest extends beyond mere industry observation."

Leo stepped forward, his gaze unwavering. "We're also interested in exploring potential collaborations – specifically, between Novotny Solutions and Dvorak Technologies. Any information you might share would be invaluable."

The polished smile flickered, a subtle, almost imperceptible shift in Novotny's composure. He quickly regained his control. "Dvorak and I have partnered on various ventures over the years. Standard industry procedure."

"Including any related to Adrian Varga?" Maggie interjected, her voice taking on a slightly sharper edge.

A muscle in Novotny's jaw tightened, a brief, involuntary betrayal of his inner state. "Adrian's work was certainly groundbreaking, but ultimately unsustainable. I personally cautioned him about the inherent risks."

Leo and Maggie exchanged a quick, knowing glance. They had struck a nerve, a vulnerability in Novotny's carefully constructed façade.

Before they could press further, Novotny abruptly stood, effectively terminating the meeting. "If you'll excuse me, a prior engagement requires my attention. My assistant will see you out."

Outside Novotny's office, Maggie turned to Leo, her voice low and urgent. "He's definitely concealing something."

"Agreed," Leo said grimly. "But we still lack concrete evidence. We need to intensify our focus on their collaboration – and expose the full scope of 'Balance Keeper.'"

That evening, back in the familiar, cluttered sanctuary of Leo's office, they immersed themselves in the documents Maggie had acquired. Among them, a series of emails detailing a joint venture between Novotny Solutions and Dvorak Technologies – the project codenamed "Balance Keeper."

"This could be the breakthrough we've been waiting for," Maggie murmured, her voice filled with a mixture of excitement and apprehension. "If we can definitively link this project to Adrian's murder, we'll have the proof we need."

"But how do we establish that *direct* link?" Leo countered, his voice laced with frustration. "Without concrete evidence, it remains circumstantial, easily refuted."

Maggie paused, considering their options. "Perhaps it's time for another calculated risk. We confront Novotny – present him with this information. Force him to react, to reveal something."

Leo shook his head firmly. "That's too dangerous, given what we now suspect. He's already demonstrated a willingness to eliminate perceived threats. We need a different approach. Something that targets his Capricorn vulnerabilities – his need for control, his meticulous planning." He began to pace, his mind formulating a new strategy.

Before their next move could be solidified, Leo's phone vibrated. Another anonymous text: "The scales tip soon. Choose wisely."

Maggie read the message over his shoulder, a knot of worry tightening in her chest. "What does that even mean?"

"It means our time is running out," Leo replied, his voice heavy with a sense of impending urgency. "Whoever is sending these messages is growing impatient – and we're caught in the middle."

The weight of the case, the constant pressure, the sense of being manipulated, began to take its toll. As the hours passed, Leo became increasingly introspective. Maggie, sensing his shift, waited until they were alone.

She spoke softly.

He look at her.

"Cases like this, where trust is broken...I think of her. Of my inability to protect her." He turned his gaze towards the window, his silhouette framed by the city lights.

For a moment, all Leo's defenses disappear.

"I just don't want to make any more mistakes, Maggie" Leo's voice was low.

"You won't," Maggie said firmly, stepping closer. "Because we're a team. And we *will* see this through to the end."

Fueled by a renewed sense of purpose, Leo and Maggie plunged back into the digital depths of Adrian's encrypted files, seeking any previously overlooked connection between

Novotny Solutions and "Balance Keeper." The data was a dense, intricate maze, but Maggie, with a sudden sharp intake of breath, unearthed a critical piece of information.

"Look at this," she said, her voice tight with urgency, pointing to a series of emails on the screen. "They're between Adrian and someone using the alias 'Project Oversight.' And the dates... they're from just days before he died."

Leo leaned closer, his eyes quickly scanning the content. The emails revealed a heated, increasingly hostile exchange – Adrian accusing the anonymous sender of misusing confidential information related to Project Phoenix.

A muscle in Leo's jaw tightened. The careful orchestration, the manipulation... it all resonated with a chilling familiarity. *Novotny*. He could almost picture the man, a meticulous planner, operating from the shadows, pulling the strings. "If Adrian threatened to expose him, to disrupt his carefully constructed world..." he murmured, the implication hanging heavy in the air.

"But why such an elaborate, indirect approach?" Maggie wondered, her brow furrowed in thought. "Why not simply shut down the project, eliminate the threat directly?"

"Because a Capricorn, especially someone like Novotny, doesn't just react; he *strategizes*," Leo explained, his voice reflecting a grim understanding of his adversary's mindset. "It's not solely about silencing Adrian; it's about controlling the narrative, about sending a message." He envisioned Novotny, a chess master, meticulously planning each move, anticipating every possible outcome.

Their intense focus was broken by the insistent vibration of Maggie's phone. Another anonymous text: "The truth is closer than you think. Look to the stars."

Maggie showed Leo the message, her expression a mix of frustration and bewilderment. "Another cryptic Zodiac message? What is this, some kind of twisted game?"

"Perhaps," Leo mused, his fingers tapping a thoughtful rhythm on the table. "Or perhaps someone is attempting to guide us, using the Zodiac as a... code. A set of veiled instructions."

"Or maybe it *is* genuine help," Maggie offered, a sliver of hope in her voice. "Could 'look to the stars' be a literal instruction? Referring to someone's astrological sign?"

Leo's gaze sharpened. Novotny, the calculated Capricorn, was an obvious suspect, but a persistent, nagging doubt remained. "Is it possible there's another player involved? Someone operating just beyond our current field of vision?"

Their next move was clear: they needed to talk to Lukáš Horák again, hoping he could shed light on the mysterious "Project Oversight" alias. They found him at his safehouse later that afternoon, his hands visibly trembling as he clutched a cup of tea. *Virgo under pressure*, Leo thought, noting the man's anxiety.

"You've found something," Lukáš stated, his voice a low, nervous murmur, his eyes darting between them.

"We have," Maggie confirmed, showing him the printed emails. "Do you recognize this account?"

Lukáš hesitated, then nodded slowly. "It... it's the same alias I used. When I leaked the information. But I swear, I stopped after Adrian confronted me."

Leo studied him intently, observing his behavior, looking for the subtle cues that might reveal more than his words. Virgos were detail-oriented and adaptable, but also prone to guilt and anxiety when caught in a compromising situation. "Did anyone else have access to your account?"

"No," Lukáš insisted, then paused, his voice dropping to a near whisper. "But... someone *knew* about it. Someone approached me... after Adrian died."

"Who?" Maggie pressed, her voice sharp and insistent.

Lukáš swallowed hard. "Novotny. He said... he could offer me protection. If I cooperated."

A look of grim understanding passed between Leo and Maggie. The puzzle pieces were falling into place, forming an increasingly disturbing picture.

"Novotny's playing a complex game," Leo stated, his voice hard. "Using Lukáš as a pawn, while simultaneously diverting suspicion from himself... and perhaps from Dvorak as well."

"But why frame Lukáš in the first place?" Maggie asked, her voice laced with frustration.

"To maintain control," Leo replied, a dark understanding in his eyes. "By creating confusion, by making us question everyone, he keeps us off balance, keeps us from seeing the bigger picture." *Classic Capricorn strategy*, he thought.

As they left Lukáš's safehouse, the need for concrete evidence pressed down on them. "We need something undeniable, Leo," Maggie said, her voice filled with urgency. "Something that definitively links Novotny to Adrian's murder."

"I know," Leo replied, his gaze distant, his mind already formulating a plan. "And I have a feeling where we might find it."

A sense of foreboding, a sense of returning to the heart of darkness, settled over them as they returned to Adrian's apartment that evening, the scene of the crime. Despite previous forensic examinations, Leo felt a persistent intuition, a belief that a crucial piece of evidence remained hidden, overlooked.

"A Capricorn, even in the midst of chaos, might leave a subtle trace," Leo murmured, his eyes scanning the room with meticulous care. "A behavioral signature, a reflection of their need for order and control."

Maggie nodded, joining the search. They moved through the disarray, a synchronized effort born of shared purpose and determination. It was Maggie who spotted it – a faint glint of metal beneath the sofa, partially obscured by dust. A small, almost insignificant-looking USB drive.

"What's this?" she asked, holding it up for Leo to examine.

Leo took the drive, turning it over in his hands. "Let's find out."

Back in the familiar, cluttered sanctuary of Leo's office, the USB drive yielded its secrets. Encrypted messages between Novotny and an unidentified individual discussing Adrian's project, financial records tracing to offshore accounts, and, most damningly, a recording of Novotny himself admitting to orchestrating Adrian's sabotage.

"This is it," Maggie breathed, a tremor of excitement and relief in her voice. "This is undeniable proof of Novotny's involvement."

"Involvement, yes," Leo corrected, his expression still grave. "But not necessarily *sole* responsibility. The chain of command could still extend further. Dvorak might still be involved, a willing – or unwilling – participant."

Maggie frowned. "So, what now?"

"Now," Leo said, his eyes hardening with resolve, "we dig deeper. We find out who Novotny was communicating with, and we expose the *entire* network of deceit." He knew they were close, but the final confrontation, the final unveiling of the truth, was yet to come. The scales of justice were poised, waiting to be tipped. He looked and Maggie and said. "Are you ready?"

The sleek, modern interior of Novotny Solutions felt like a battleground as Leo and Maggie returned, the USB drive containing the incriminating evidence a weapon in their arsenal. They were no longer seeking clues; they were seeking a confession.

Novotny greeted them with his usual polished smile, but this time, Leo detected a flicker of apprehension, a subtle tension behind the Capricorn's mask of control. The carefully constructed façade was beginning to show cracks.

"Back so soon?" Novotny inquired smoothly, gesturing for them to sit. "Have you, perhaps, changed your minds about my lack of involvement?"

Leo ignored the veiled sarcasm, placing the USB drive squarely on Novotny's pristine desk, the small device holding the weight of their accusations. "We recovered this from Adrian's apartment. I believe you're familiar with its contents."

Novotny's smile wavered, a fleeting, almost imperceptible tremor before he regained his composure. His voice, however, remained steady. "I have no idea what that is. I've never seen it before."

Maggie leaned forward, her voice sharp, cutting through the pretense. "It contains encrypted communications between you and an unidentified individual, discussing Adrian's project. Financial records linking to offshore accounts. And a recording – *your* voice, Mr. Novotny – admitting to orchestrating the sabotage."

A muscle in Novotny's jaw twitched, a subtle but telling sign of his internal struggle. He recovered quickly, his Capricorn pragmatism kicking in. "Even if that were authentic – and I'm not admitting that it is – it doesn't prove I was responsible for his *death*."

"No," Leo agreed, his voice low and controlled. "But it establishes a clear motive – and the means to carry out the plan." He watched Novotny intently, searching for any further sign of weakness, any crack in his carefully constructed defenses.

Novotny hesitated, then let out a calculated sigh, a performance of weary resignation. "Alright. I admit I wasn't entirely truthful before. Adrian's project posed a significant threat to my company's interests. But I would *never* resort to murder."

"Yet someone *did*," Maggie countered, her voice unwavering. "And the evidence points directly to you."

Novotny's expression shifted, a flicker of anger replacing the mask of composure. "If you're accusing me of murder, you'd better have irrefutable proof."

"We're getting closer," Leo replied, his voice a low, steady threat. "And when we do uncover the *full* truth, you'll wish you'd cooperated from the beginning."

As they continued to press Novotny, Leo observed subtle shifts in his behavior – the tightened jaw, the slightly accelerated breathing, the carefully chosen words. *The Capricorn under pressure*, he thought, noting how the man's outward calm was beginning to crumble, revealing glimpses of the ruthless pragmatism and desperation beneath.

"You think you understand what's at stake here?" Novotny snapped, his voice rising slightly, a crack in his controlled demeanor. "You have no *idea*. Adrian was meddling with forces he didn't comprehend. If he hadn't pushed so hard, none of this would have happened."

"What forces?" Maggie pressed, her voice sharp and insistent.

Novotny hesitated, then shook his head, his eyes hardening with a mixture of defiance and fear. "I'm not saying anything further without legal counsel."

Leo and Maggie exchanged a quick, knowing glance. They had reached an impasse, but not before uncovering a significant revelation. Novotny's carefully constructed defenses had momentarily crumbled, revealing a glimpse of something darker, something more complex than they had initially anticipated. He knew *more*.

Back in the familiar clutter of Leo's office, amidst the corkboard and scattered files, they re-examined the evidence, piecing together the timeline, analyzing Novotny's reactions, trying to decipher his cryptic statement.

JUSTICE IN THE SHADOWS 133

"So, Novotny admits to orchestrating the sabotage," Maggie mused, tapping a pen against her notebook. "But he's still holding something back. What did he mean by 'forces' Adrian didn't understand?"

"It suggests a larger conspiracy," Leo replied, his voice thoughtful. "Something beyond corporate rivalry. Something Novotny himself might be afraid of." He considered the possibilities, the complex interplay of personalities and motivations.

"But who's ultimately in control?" Maggie pressed. "Is it Dvorak? Is it Novotny? Or is it someone else entirely?"

"We need to find out," Leo said, his voice filled with a renewed determination. "And we need to consider all possibilities – even the ones that seem unlikely." He thought of Evan, the secretive Scorpio, and his potential for vengeance. He thought of Clara, and her initial deception. He thought of everyone they had encountered, everyone connected to Adrian, everyone with a potential motive.

The weight to know grew.

Chapter 12

The weight of unanswered questions hung heavy in the air as Leo and Maggie convened at their usual café, the morning light casting long shadows across their table. They needed to connect the disparate pieces of the puzzle, to understand the full scope of the conspiracy surrounding Adrian's murder, and to finally expose the mastermind behind it all.

"We know Dvorak orchestrated the sabotage, and Novotny admits to facilitating it," Maggie began, her voice low and thoughtful, stirring her coffee. "But neither of them seems to be the ultimate authority. Someone else is directing them, or at least, influencing their actions."

Leo nodded, his gaze distant, his mind already analyzing the behavioral patterns, the interplay of personalities. He considered Dvorak's Leo pride and need for control, and Novotny's Capricorn pragmatism and ruthlessness. *But who*, he wondered, *could manipulate both of them?*

"Dvorak wouldn't willingly be a pawn," Leo mused. "He's too proud, too concerned with his own image. And Novotny is too calculating to act without a clear advantage, a guaranteed outcome." He paused, considering the possibilities. "There has to be a hidden player, someone we haven't fully considered."

"But who?" Maggie questioned, her brow furrowed in thought. "And how do we find them?"

"We revisit everything," Leo replied, his voice firm with resolve. "Every clue, every conversation, every interaction. We look for inconsistencies, for hidden connections, for anything that might point us in the right direction." He knew they were close, but the final piece of the puzzle remained elusive.

Their strategy led them back to Dvorak Technologies that afternoon, but this time, their approach was different. Instead of posing as auditors, they adopted a more covert approach, seeking to observe, to listen, to gather information without drawing attention to themselves. Maggie, leveraging her journalistic skills, arranged for them to access the building as part of a "documentary crew" filming a piece on innovative tech companies.

Inside, the atmosphere was, as always, one of controlled efficiency. Employees moved with a quiet, almost robotic precision, their attention seemingly glued to the screens before them. But beneath the surface, Leo sensed a current of unease, a subtle tension that hadn't been present during their previous visits.

They spent hours observing the interactions between employees, listening to snippets of conversations, searching for any clue that might shed light on the inner workings of Dvorak Technologies, on the relationships between its key players. Leo, with his keen understanding of human behavior, focused on the subtle cues – body language, facial expressions, tone of voice – looking for any sign of deception, any hint of hidden knowledge.

It was Maggie who made the first breakthrough. While filming a seemingly innocuous scene in the company cafeteria, she overheard a conversation between two employees, their voices low and conspiratorial.

"Did you hear about the meeting last night?" one of them said. "Dvorak and Novotny... they were arguing. It sounded... intense."

"I heard," the other replied. "Something about 'Balance Keeper.' About 'damage control.' It's getting... scary."

Leo, who had been observing from a distance, felt a surge of adrenaline. *Dvorak and Novotny, arguing. Damage control.* This was a significant development, a crack in the carefully constructed façade of their alliance.

They needed to learn more.

Later that evening, back in the familiar clutter of Leo's office, they reviewed their findings, piecing together the fragments of information they had gathered.

"Dvorak and Novotny are at odds," Maggie said, her voice filled with a mixture of excitement and apprehension. "Something has shifted in their relationship. Something related to 'Balance Keeper.'"

"It's possible that Novotny is losing control," Leo mused. "Or perhaps Dvorak is starting to question his role in the conspiracy. Either way, it creates an opportunity for us." He tapped a finger on the corkboard, his mind racing.

Before they could formulate a new plan, Leo's phone vibrated. Another anonymous text: "The scales tip soon. Choose wisely."

Maggie read the message over his shoulder, her brow furrowed in concern. "What is that supposed to mean?"

"It means we're running out of time," Leo said.

As nigth comes.

Leo was lost in his thought, thinking about his sister.

Maggie approach him, she look at him and said.

"We are closer than never, we will get them." she said

Leo, nodded.

With the anonymous message – "Look to the stars" – echoing in their minds, Leo and Maggie decided to re-examine Adrian's digital footprint, specifically focusing on any potential connections between Dvorak Technologies and "Balance Keeper." They returned to the encrypted files, hoping to uncover a previously overlooked detail, a hidden link.

Maggie, navigating the complex data streams, suddenly paused, her eyes widening. "Here," she said, her voice sharp with urgency. "These emails... they're between Adrian and someone using the alias 'Project Oversight.' And the dates... they're from just days before he died."

Leo leaned closer, his gaze fixed on the screen. The emails revealed a tense, increasingly hostile exchange – Adrian accusing the anonymous sender of misusing confidential information related to Project Phoenix.

Leo's jaw clenched. The careful planning, the manipulation, the indirect approach... it all pointed to Dvorak's influence. *Leo*. The need for dominance, the willingness to eliminate any perceived threat... "If Adrian threatened his position, his carefully constructed world..." he murmured, the implication clear.

"But why such a convoluted strategy?" Maggie wondered, her brow furrowed. "Why not simply shut down the project, remove the threat directly?"

"Because a Leo, especially someone like Dvorak, doesn't just react; he *orchestrates*," Leo explained, his voice reflecting a grim understanding of his adversary's mindset. "It's not solely about silencing Adrian; it's about making a statement, about demonstrating his power and control." He pictured Dvorak, a master manipulator, enjoying the unfolding chaos from a safe distance, relishing his ability to control events.

Their intense focus was broken by the insistent vibration of Maggie's phone. Another anonymous text: "The truth is closer than you think. Look to the stars."

Maggie showed Leo the message, her expression a mix of frustration and intrigue. "Another Zodiac riddle? Is this a game to whoever is behind this?"

"Perhaps," Leo mused, his fingers tapping a thoughtful rhythm on the table. "Or perhaps someone is attempting to guide us, using the Zodiac as a... language. A coded message."

"Or maybe it *is* a genuine offer of help," Maggie suggested, a sliver of hope in her voice. "Could 'look to the stars' be a literal instruction? Referring to someone's astrological sign?"

Leo's gaze sharpened. Dvorak, the domineering Leo, was the primary suspect, but a persistent, nagging doubt remained. "Could there be another player involved? Someone we haven't fully considered, someone operating just beyond our current understanding?" He considered the possibilities, the complex interplay of personalities and motivations.

Seeking further insight into the "Project Oversight" alias, they decided to revisit Lukáš Horák that afternoon. They found him at his safehouse, his hands visibly trembling as he clutched a cup of tea, a clear manifestation of a Virgo under immense stress.

"You've discovered something," he stated, his voice a low, nervous murmur, his eyes darting between them.

"We have," Maggie confirmed, showing him the printed emails. "Do you recognize this account?"

Lukáš hesitated, then nodded slowly, his gaze downcast. "It... it's the same alias I used. When I leaked the information. But I swear, I stopped after Adrian confronted me."

Leo studied him intently, observing his behavior, looking for the subtle cues that might reveal more than his words. Virgos were detail-oriented and adaptable, but also prone to anxiety and guilt when caught in a compromising situation. "Did anyone else have access to your account?"

"No," Lukáš insisted, then paused, his voice dropping to a near whisper. "But... someone *knew* about it. Someone approached me... after Adrian died."

"Who?" Maggie pressed, her voice sharp and insistent.

Lukáš swallowed hard, his eyes filled with a mixture of fear and resignation. "Dvorak. He said... he could offer me protection. If I cooperated."

A look of grim understanding passed between Leo and Maggie. The puzzle pieces were falling into place, forming an increasingly disturbing picture.

"Dvorak's playing a complex game," Leo stated, his voice hard, his eyes reflecting a cold determination. "Using Lukáš as a pawn, while simultaneously distancing himself from the crime." He considered Dvorak's Leo traits – the need for control, the manipulation, the willingness to exploit others.

"But what was his motive for originally involving Lukas?" said Maggie.

Leo look at her "Control"

The urgency of their task pressed down on them as they left Lukáš's safehouse. "We need concrete evidence, Leo," Maggie said, her voice filled with determination. "Something that definitively links Dvorak to Adrian's murder, something undeniable."

"I know," Leo replied, his gaze distant, his mind already formulating a plan. "And I have a strong intuition where we might find it."

A sense of returning to the heart of darkness, to the source of the chaos, enveloped them as they returned to Adrian's apartment that evening. Despite previous forensic examinations, Leo felt a persistent belief that a crucial piece of evidence remained hidden, overlooked.

"A Leo, even in orchestrating a crime, might leave a subtle trace," Leo murmured, his eyes scanning the room with meticulous care. "A touch of ego, a behavioral signature, something reflecting his need for control and his desire for recognition."

Maggie nodded, joining the search. They moved through the disarray, a synchronized effort born of shared purpose and unwavering resolve. It was Maggie who spotted it – a faint glint of metal beneath the sofa, partially obscured by dust and shadow. A small, almost insignificant-looking USB drive.

"What's this?" she asked, holding it up for Leo to examine.

Leo took the drive, turning it over in his hands. "Let's find out."

Back in the familiar, cluttered sanctuary of Leo's office, the USB drive yielded its secrets. Encrypted messages between Dvorak and an unidentified individual discussing Adrian's project, financial records tracing to offshore accounts, and, most damningly, a recording of Dvorak himself admitting to orchestrating Adrian's sabotage.

"This is it," Maggie breathed, a tremor of excitement and relief in her voice. "This is undeniable proof of Dvorak's direct involvement."

"Involvement, yes," Leo corrected, his expression still grave. "But not necessarily *sole* responsibility. It's still possible someone else was involved, that Dvorak was, perhaps, a powerful pawn in a larger game." He considered the possibilities, the complex interplay of personalities and motivations.

Maggie frowned, her mind racing. "You still suspect Novotny?"

"Or someone else entirely," Leo replied. "We can't afford to narrow our focus too soon. We need to keep digging, keep analyzing, until we uncover the *full* truth."

As the night drew on, their conversation quieted, replaced by a shared sense of purpose and a quiet understanding. The weight of the case, the echoes of past failures, pressed down on Leo, but Maggie's presence, her unwavering support, provided a much-needed anchor. He knew they were close, but the final confrontation, the final unraveling of the truth, was yet to come.

Leo finally said. "We are so close now."

Chapter 13

The stalemate with Dvorak, his near-confession and subsequent refusal to speak, left Leo and Maggie frustrated, but also with a renewed sense of urgency. They knew they were close to uncovering the full truth, but a crucial piece was still missing. They needed to find out what "forces" Adrian had been meddling with, what secret he had threatened to expose.

Their investigation took them back to where it all began: Adrian's meticulously organized apartment. This time, however, they weren't searching for physical clues or digital footprints. They were searching for something more intangible – a connection, a relationship, a hint of something that might have been overlooked in the initial chaos.

"We need to think like Adrian," Leo said, his gaze sweeping across the room, taking in the familiar details – the books, the research papers, the intricate models of balanced structures. "What was he obsessed with? What was he *afraid* of?" He wasn't just looking at the physical objects; he was trying to understand Adrian's mind, his motivations, his fears.

Maggie, meanwhile, focused on Adrian's personal belongings – his journals, his letters, his photographs. She was searching for a human connection, a glimpse into his personal life that might shed light on his professional struggles.

Hours passed, and the apartment remained stubbornly silent, revealing nothing new. The initial excitement of the investigation had faded, replaced by a growing sense of frustration.

It was Maggie who finally broke the silence. "Look at this," she said, her voice a mixture of surprise and confusion. She held up a photograph, a seemingly innocuous image of Adrian at a conference, standing next to a group of people.

Leo took the photograph, his eyes scanning the faces. He recognized Dvorak and Novotny, their expressions carefully neutral, their body language betraying a hint of tension. But there was another man in the photograph, a man he didn't recognize. A man who seemed... out of place.

"Who is this?" Leo asked, pointing to the unfamiliar figure.

Maggie turned the photograph over, revealing a handwritten inscription on the back: "Adrian, with Professor Albin Varga and colleagues, Prague Tech Conference, 2023."

"Professor Albin Varga," Maggie murmured. "Could he be related to Adrian? A family member?"

Leo's mind raced. The name resonated with a faint familiarity, a forgotten detail from the initial investigation. He quickly accessed the case files on his laptop, searching for any mention of Albin Varga.

"Here," he said, his voice rising with excitement. "Albin Varga. Adrian's uncle. A professor of... theoretical physics. Specializing in... balance and equilibrium." He looked up at Maggie, his eyes widening. "The same concepts Adrian was obsessed with. The same concepts reflected in the killer's 'Balance Keeper' symbol."

"But what's the connection?" Maggie asked, her brow furrowed in thought. "Why would Adrian's uncle be involved in his murder?"

"I don't know," Leo admitted. "But there's something... unsettling about this photograph. Something about the way Albin Varga is looking at Adrian. It's not... avuncular. It's... something else." He studied the photograph again, focusing on Albin Varga's expression, his body language. He was a Libra, Leo recalled, a sign associated with balance, harmony, and... justice. But there was something in his eyes, a coldness, a detachment, that didn't fit the typical Libra profile.

"We need to find Albin Varga," Leo said, his voice firm with resolve. "He might be the silent witness, the missing piece of this puzzle."

He paused, his gaze settling on Maggie. "We need to be careful, though. If Albin Varga *is* involved, he's likely to be as dangerous as Dvorak and Novotny. Perhaps... even more so." He knew they were stepping into uncharted territory, confronting an unknown entity, a hidden mastermind who might hold the key to unlocking the entire conspiracy.

Maggie looked at him.

"I know." she said.

Leo, stood up.

"Let's find him"

Their renewed investigation began, once again, with Adrian's digital archive. Leo and Maggie sought any previously overlooked connection between Novotny Solutions, Dvorak Technologies, and the cryptic "Balance Keeper." The encrypted files were a labyrinth, but Maggie, with a sudden sharp intake of breath, discovered a critical detail.

"These emails," she said, her voice a mix of urgency and disbelief, "they're between Adrian and someone using the alias 'Project Oversight.' And the dates... they're from just days before he died."

Leo leaned closer, his eyes quickly scanning the content. The emails revealed a tense, increasingly hostile exchange – Adrian accusing the anonymous sender of misusing confidential Project Phoenix information.

Leo's jaw clenched. The careful orchestration, the manipulation, the indirect approach... Now, with fresh eyes, it all seemed to point to Novotny, *The Capricorn*. He was known to take extreme measures. "If Adrian was a liability..." he murmured, the implication hanging heavy in the air.

"But why such an elaborate scheme?" Maggie wondered, her brow furrowed. "Why not simply shut down the project, eliminate the threat directly?"

"Because a Capricorn, particularly someone like Novotny, doesn't just react; he *controls*," Leo explained, his voice reflecting a grim understanding. "It's not solely about silencing Adrian; it's about sending a message, about demonstrating his power." He pictured Novotny, a meticulous planner, orchestrating events from afar.

Their focus was interrupted by the vibration of Maggie's phone. Another anonymous text: "The truth is closer than you think. Look to the stars."

Maggie showed Leo the message, her expression a mixture of frustration and intrigue. "Another Zodiac riddle? Is this a game to them?"

"Perhaps," Leo mused, his fingers tapping a thoughtful rhythm on the table. "Or perhaps someone is attempting to guide us, using the Zodiac as a... code."

"Or maybe it *is* a genuine offer of help," Maggie suggested, a sliver of hope in her voice. "Could 'look to the stars' be literal? Referring to someone's astrological sign?"

Leo's gaze sharpened. Novotny, the calculated Capricorn, was an obvious suspect, but a persistent, nagging doubt remained. "Is it possible there's another player involved? Someone we haven't fully considered, someone operating just beyond our current understanding?" He ran through the possibilities in his head.

With the "Project Oversight" alias still a mystery, they decided to revisit Lukáš Horák that afternoon. They found him at his safehouse, his hands visibly trembling as he held a cup of tea. The anxieties of a Virgo under pressure, Leo observed.

"You've discovered something," he stated, his voice a low, nervous murmur, his eyes darting between them.

"We have," Maggie confirmed, showing him the printed emails. "Do you recognize this account?"

Lukáš hesitated, then nodded slowly, his gaze downcast. "It... it's the same alias I used. When I leaked the information. But I swear, I stopped after Adrian confronted me."

Leo studied him intently, observing his behavior, looking for the subtle cues that might reveal more than his words. Virgos were detail-oriented and adaptable, but also prone to guilt and anxiety when caught in a compromising situation. "Did anyone else have access to your account?"

"No," Lukáš insisted, then paused, his voice dropping to a near whisper. "But... someone *knew* about it. Someone approached me... after Adrian died."

"Who?" Maggie pressed, her voice sharp and insistent.

Lukáš swallowed hard. "Novotny. He said... he could offer me protection. If I cooperated."

A look of grim understanding passed between Leo and Maggie. They had another confirmation, another piece of the puzzle.

"Novotny's playing a complex game," Leo stated, his voice hard. "Using Lukáš as a pawn, while simultaneously trying to cover all tracks"

"But why use Lukas at all?" Maggie asked.

"Control and efficiency" Leo replied.

The need for undeniable evidence weighed heavily on them as they left Lukáš's safehouse. "We need something concrete, Leo," Maggie said, her voice filled with urgency. "Something that definitively links Novotny to Adrian's murder."

"I know," Leo replied, his gaze distant, his mind already formulating a plan. "And there might be something at the crime scene."

A sense of foreboding, a sense of returning to the heart of darkness, enveloped them as they returned to Adrian's apartment that evening. Despite previous forensic examinations, and their own searches, Leo felt a persistent intuition, a belief that a crucial piece of evidence remained – overlooked, perhaps, in the initial chaos.

"A Capricorn, even in the midst of orchestrating a crime, might leave a subtle trace," Leo murmured, his eyes scanning the room with meticulous care. "A behavioral signature, something reflecting their need for order."

Maggie nodded, joining the search. It was Maggie who spotted it – a faint glint of metal beneath the sofa, partially obscured by dust. A small USB drive.

"What's this?" she asked.

Leo took the drive. "Let's find out."

Back in Leo's office, the USB drive revealed its secrets: encrypted messages between *Novotny* and an unknown party, discussing Adrian's project; financial records; and the recording of Novotny.

"This proves Novotny's involvement," Maggie said, excitement mixing with a renewed sense of gravity.

"Involvement, yes," Leo agreed, his expression serious. "But not necessarily *sole* responsibility. It still doesn't fully explain *why*. Or who else might be involved." He knew they were close, but the complete picture, the full extent of the conspiracy, remained just beyond their grasp.

The weight of un answered questions, made Leo get quiet.

Maggie knew he was caring to much.

"We will get to the end of it, we are closer than ever" she reassured him.

The sleek, modern interior of Novotny Solutions felt charged with a palpable tension as Leo and Maggie returned, the incriminating USB drive a silent weapon in their quest for justice. They were no longer seeking clues; they were seeking a confession, a final unraveling of the carefully constructed web of deceit.

Novotny greeted them with his usual polished smile, but behind the Capricorn's mask of control, Leo detected a flicker of apprehension, a subtle unease. The carefully constructed façade was beginning to show strain.

"Back so soon?" Novotny inquired smoothly, gesturing for them to sit. "Have you, perhaps, reconsidered my lack of involvement?"

Leo ignored the feigned innocence, placing the USB drive squarely on Novotny's pristine desk, a silent accusation. "We recovered this from Adrian's apartment. I believe you're familiar with its contents."

Novotny's smile vanished, replaced by a carefully controlled expression of neutrality. His voice, however, remained steady. "I have no idea what that is. I've never seen it before."

Maggie leaned forward, her voice sharp, cutting through the pretense like a knife. "It contains encrypted communications between you and an unidentified individual, discussing Adrian's project. Financial records linking to offshore accounts. And a recording – *your* voice, Mr. Novotny – admitting to orchestrating the sabotage."

A muscle in Novotny's jaw twitched, a subtle but telling betrayal of his internal struggle. He recovered quickly, his Capricorn pragmatism and need for control reasserting themselves. "Even if that were authentic – and I'm not admitting that it is – it doesn't prove I was responsible for his *death*."

"No," Leo agreed, his voice low and controlled. "But it establishes a clear motive – and the means to carry out the plan." He watched Novotny intently, searching for any further sign of weakness, any crack in his carefully constructed defenses.

Novotny hesitated, then let out a calculated sigh, a performance of weary resignation. "Alright, I admit I wasn't entirely truthful before. Adrian's project posed a significant threat to my company's interests. But I would *never* resort to murder."

"Yet someone *did*," Maggie countered, her voice unwavering. "And the evidence points directly to you."

Novotny's expression shifted, a flicker of anger replacing the mask of composure. "If you're accusing me of murder, you'd better have irrefutable proof."

"We're getting closer," Leo replied, his voice a low, steady threat. "And when we uncover the *full* truth, you'll wish you'd cooperated from the beginning."

As they continued to press Novotny, Leo observed subtle shifts in his behavior – the tightened jaw, the slightly accelerated breathing, the carefully chosen words, the way his hands subtly clenched. *The Capricorn under pressure*, he thought, noting how the man's outward calm was beginning to crumble, revealing glimpses of the ruthless determination and desperation beneath.

"You think you understand what's at stake here?" Novotny snapped, his voice rising slightly, a crack in his controlled demeanor. "You have no *idea*. Adrian was meddling with forces he didn't comprehend. If he hadn't pushed so hard, none of this would have happened."

"What forces?" Maggie pressed, her voice sharp and insistent.

Novotny hesitated, then shook his head, his eyes hardening with a mixture of defiance and fear. "I'm not saying anything further without legal counsel." The classic Capricorn retreat – build a wall, protect the secrets, maintain control at all costs.

Leo and Maggie exchanged a quick, knowing glance. They had reached an impasse, a stalemate. But Novotny's outburst, his near-confession, had revealed a crucial piece of the puzzle. There was *more* to the story, a deeper, darker secret that Adrian had threatened to expose, a secret that Novotny was desperate to protect.

Later, in the familiar, almost comforting clutter of Leo's office, they re-examined the evidence, piecing together the timeline, analyzing Novotny's reactions, trying to decipher his cryptic statement.

They reviewed and reviewed.

"What are this forces, he was talking about?" Maggie said.

Leo shook is head.

Maggie stood up.

"We need to find out," she said, her voice firm. "We need to understand what Adrian uncovered, what forces he was playing with. And we need to do it before anyone else gets hurt."

Leo nodded, his mind already racing, formulating a new plan. "We go back to the beginning," he said, his voice filled with a renewed determination. "We re-examine everything. Every clue, every conversation, every connection. We leave no stone unturned." He knew the truth was out there, hidden in the shadows, waiting to be revealed. The final confrontation was approaching, and they needed to be ready.

Chapter 14

With Novotny's cryptic warning – "forces he didn't understand" – hanging heavy in the air, Leo and Maggie knew they were missing a crucial piece of the puzzle. The confrontation had yielded an admission of guilt for the sabotage, but the *why* behind Adrian's murder remained elusive, shrouded in a deeper, more unsettling mystery.

They returned to Leo's office, the familiar clutter of files, photographs, and the ever-present corkboard offering a strange sense of comfort in the face of the growing uncertainty. They needed to re-examine everything, to look beyond the obvious suspects, to consider the possibility of an unseen hand manipulating events from the shadows.

"Novotny and Dvorak are both involved, that much is clear," Maggie said, her voice low and thoughtful, pacing the room. "But neither of them seems to be the ultimate mastermind. Dvorak is too proud, too focused on his own image. And Novotny... he's calculating, yes, but he also seemed genuinely *afraid* when he mentioned those 'forces.'"

Leo nodded, his gaze fixed on the corkboard, his mind sifting through the evidence, analyzing the personalities involved, searching for a pattern, a connection, that might have been overlooked. He thought of Dvorak's Leo need for control, of Novotny's Capricorn pragmatism, of Evan's Scorpio intensity, of Lukáš's Virgo anxiety... and of Adrian, the brilliant, driven Gemini who had stumbled onto something dangerous.

"We need to go back to Adrian's research," Leo said, his voice firm with resolve. "Not just Project Phoenix, but *everything* he was working on. There has to be a clue there, something that will explain Novotny's fear, Dvorak's involvement, and the ultimate motive for Adrian's murder."

They spent hours poring over Adrian's files, his notes, his research papers, his emails. They delved into his academic background, his professional collaborations, his personal life. They were searching for anything that might shed light on the "forces" Novotny had alluded to, anything that might reveal the hidden mastermind behind the conspiracy.

It was Maggie who made the first breakthrough. While examining Adrian's academic publications, she discovered a series of articles co-authored with a Professor Albin Varga – Adrian's uncle, the theoretical physicist specializing in balance and equilibrium.

"Leo, look at this," she said, her voice filled with a mixture of excitement and apprehension. "Adrian collaborated extensively with his uncle. And their research... it goes far beyond Project Phoenix. It delves into... some pretty esoteric concepts."

Leo joined her, his eyes scanning the titles of the articles: "The Symmetry of Chaos," "Harnessing Zero-Point Energy," "The Unified Field Theory and its Implications for Technological Advancement." These were not the typical topics of a cybersecurity expert.

"This is... different," Leo murmured, his brow furrowed in thought. "This is far more theoretical, more... fundamental. What was Adrian *really* working on?" He considered the implications, the potential for groundbreaking discoveries, for disruptive technologies... for dangerous secrets.

They delved deeper into Albin Varga's research, discovering a complex and often controversial body of work that explored the very foundations of reality, the nature of energy, the interconnectedness of all things. Varga's theories, while brilliant, were also considered radical, even fringe, by many in the scientific community.

"This is what Novotny was talking about," Leo said, his voice filled with a growing sense of unease. "These 'forces'... they're not just corporate rivals or political enemies. They're... something else entirely. Something related to Adrian's uncle's research."

"But what?" Maggie asked, her voice a whisper. "What could be so dangerous, so valuable, that it would lead to Adrian's murder?"

Leo shook his head, his mind racing. "I don't know," he admitted. "But I have a feeling we're about to find out." He looked at Maggie, his eyes filled with a mixture of apprehension and determination. "We need to find Albin Varga. He might be the only one who can explain what's really going on."

He paused, his gaze settling on the photograph of Adrian and his uncle, the image that had sparked this new line of inquiry. He studied Albin Varga's face, searching for a clue, a hint of the man's true nature. *Libra*, he thought, the sign of balance, harmony, and justice. But there was something in

Varga's eyes, a coldness, a detachment, that belied the typical Libra traits. Something that suggested a hidden depth, a potential for darkness.

"We need to be careful, Maggie," Leo said, his voice low and serious. "We're stepping into unknown territory. We're dealing with forces we don't fully understand. And we might be facing an enemy far more powerful than we ever imagined." He knew the stakes were higher than ever, the danger more profound. The search for the truth had led them to the precipice of something vast and unsettling, something that could change everything.

THE DISCOVERY OF ALBIN Varga, Adrian's uncle and a fellow researcher in the esoteric field of balance and equilibrium, had thrown a new light on the case. Leo and Maggie decided their next step was to delve deeper into Albin's work, hoping to find a connection to "Balance Keeper" and Adrian's murder.

They began by revisiting Adrian's digital archive, this time specifically searching for any communication between Adrian and his uncle. The encrypted files, a labyrinth of data, slowly began to yield their secrets. Maggie, with her sharp eye for detail, unearthed a series of emails.

"Here," she said, her voice a mix of urgency and discovery. "Emails between Adrian and someone using the alias 'Project Oversight.' We assumed it was Dvorak or Novotny, but... look at the dates. They coincide with the conference where Adrian was photographed with his uncle."

Leo leaned closer, his eyes scanning the content. The emails revealed a heated, increasingly acrimonious exchange – Adrian accusing the anonymous sender of misusing confidential information, not just about Project Phoenix, but about something *more*. Something related to his uncle's research.

Leo's jaw tightened. The meticulous planning, the manipulation, the indirect approach... it could be Dvorak. But there were too many variables. *Leo*. The need for dominance, the willingness to eliminate any perceived threat... "If Adrian threatened to expose something, to disrupt Albin's research or reputation..." he murmured, the implication clear. It wasn't about corporate espionage anymore; it was something far more complex.

"But why such an elaborate scheme?" Maggie wondered, her brow furrowed. "If it *was* Dvorak, why not just discredit the research, silence Adrian directly?"

"Because a Leo, especially someone like Dvorak, doesn't just react; he *controls*," Leo explained, his voice reflecting a grim understanding. "It's not solely about silencing Adrian; it's about controlling the narrative, about making a statement." He pictured Dvorak, a master manipulator, enjoying the unfolding chaos from a safe distance. But something still didn't quite fit.

Their analysis was interrupted by the insistent vibration of Maggie's phone. Another anonymous text: "The truth is closer than you think. Look to the stars."

Maggie showed Leo the message, her expression a mix of frustration and intrigue. "Another Zodiac riddle? Is this a game to whoever is sending these?"

"Perhaps," Leo mused, his fingers tapping a thoughtful rhythm on the table. "Or perhaps someone is attempting to guide us, using the Zodiac as a... code. A set of veiled instructions."

"Or maybe it *is* genuine help," Maggie offered, a sliver of hope in her voice. "Could 'look to the stars' be a literal instruction? Referring to someone's astrological sign?"

Leo's gaze sharpened. Dvorak, the domineering Leo, was a suspect, but so was Novotny, and now... Albin Varga, a Libra. "We need to consider all possibilities," he said, his voice firm. "There might be another player involved, someone we haven't fully considered."

To gain further insight into "Project Oversight," they decided to revisit Lukáš Horák that afternoon. They found him at his safehouse, visibly shaken, his hands trembling as he held a cup of tea – a Virgo overwhelmed by anxiety and guilt.

"You've discovered something," he stated, his voice a low, nervous murmur, his eyes darting between them.

"We have," Maggie confirmed, showing him the printed emails. "Do you recognize this account?"

Lukáš hesitated, then nodded slowly, his gaze downcast. "It... it's the same alias I used. When I leaked the information. But I swear, I stopped after Adrian confronted me."

Leo studied him intently, observing his behavior. "Did anyone else have access to your account, Lukas?"

"No," Lukáš insisted, then paused, his voice dropping to a near whisper. "But... someone *knew* about it. Someone approached me... after Adrian died."

"Who?" Maggie pressed, her voice sharp and insistent.

Lukáš swallowed hard. "Dvorak," he whispered, his voice filled with fear. "He said... he could offer me protection. If I cooperated."

A look of grim understanding passed between Leo and Maggie. The puzzle pieces were shifting, reforming into a new, even more disturbing picture.

"Dvorak was using you," Leo stated, his voice hard. "But to what end? Was it simply about Novotny, or was there something more?"

"I...I don't know," Lukáš stammered. "He just said...he said it was important. That I had to do what he said."

Leaving Lukáš's safehouse.

"We need to find something to link Dvorak to Adrian's murder" Maggie said.

"I know where to start looking" Leo said.

That evening, guided by a growing sense of urgency, they returned to Adrian's apartment. Leo felt a persistent intuition, a belief that a crucial piece of evidence remained, overlooked in previous searches.

"We've focused on the digital, on the corporate," Leo murmured, his eyes scanning the room with meticulous care. "But what about the personal? What about Adrian's *life* outside of work?"

Maggie nodded, understanding his line of reasoning. They began to search again, this time focusing not on the obvious clues, but on the subtle details, the personal touches that might reveal a hidden connection.

It was Maggie who made the discovery – a small, almost unnoticeable glint of metal beneath the sofa. A USB drive, partially hidden by dust.

"What's this?" she asked, holding it up.

Leo took the drive, his heart pounding with anticipation. "Let's find out."

Back in Leo's office, the USB drive revealed its secrets: encrypted messages, financial transactions, and a recording. But these weren't between Dvorak and Novotny. They were between Dvorak and... *someone else*. Someone identified only as "A.V."

Leo and Maggie exchanged a look of stunned realization. *A.V.* Albin Varga.

"This changes everything," Maggie breathed, her voice filled with a mixture of excitement and dread. "This could be the missing link. The unseen hand."

"But what was Albin Varga's role?" Leo wondered aloud, his mind racing. "Was he working *with* Dvorak? Or was he... controlling him?" He considered the implications, the possibility that they had been chasing the wrong mastermind all along. The scales of justice were shifting, revealing a new, even more complex and dangerous truth. He stood up, "We need to find him."

THE DISCOVERY OF THE USB drive, with its incriminating messages between Dvorak and *Albin Varga*, had shifted the entire landscape of the case. Leo and Maggie now faced a choice: confront Dvorak with this new evidence, or seek out Albin Varga directly. The anonymous text – "The scales tip soon" – added a sense of urgency to their decision.

They decided on a two-pronged approach. Maggie would attempt to locate Albin Varga, using her journalistic contacts and research skills. Leo, meanwhile, would confront Dvorak, not with accusations, but with a carefully crafted strategy designed to expose the truth.

Leo returned to Dvorak Technologies alone. He needed to see Dvorak's reaction, to gauge his response to this new, unexpected development. He needed to understand the dynamic between Dvorak and Albin Varga, to uncover the *true* mastermind behind Adrian's murder.

The atmosphere in Dvorak's office was thick with tension. The opulent surroundings, the panoramic view of Prague, seemed to mock the grim reality of the situation. Dvorak, the proud Leo, greeted Leo with a forced smile, his eyes betraying a flicker of anxiety.

"Detective Maxwell," Dvorak said, his voice smooth but strained. "To what do I owe this... unexpected visit?"

Leo didn't waste time with pleasantries. He held up the USB drive, the small device containing the damning evidence. "We've analyzed the contents of this drive, Mr. Dvorak. We know about your communications with... Albin Varga."

Dvorak's carefully constructed façade crumbled. The color drained from his face, his eyes widening in shock and disbelief. He opened his mouth to speak, but no words came out. The proud Leo, accustomed to controlling every situation, was visibly shaken.

"We know about 'Balance Keeper,'" Leo continued, his voice low and steady. "We know about Adrian's sabotage. And we know about your involvement in his... silencing." He paused, letting his words sink in. "What we *don't* know is... *why*."

Dvorak finally found his voice, but it was a mere whisper. "Albin... he..." He stopped, unable to continue.

"He what, Mr. Dvorak?" Leo pressed, his gaze unwavering. "Did he order you to kill Adrian? Was he the one pulling the strings?"

Dvorak looked away, his gaze fixed on the cityscape outside, his expression a mixture of fear and... something else. Regret? Guilt? Resignation?

"He... he said it was necessary," Dvorak finally said, his voice barely audible. "He said Adrian was a threat. To his research... to *everything*."

"And you believed him?" Leo asked, his voice laced with a hint of disbelief.

Dvorak nodded slowly. "He... he has a way of... convincing people. He's... brilliant. Charismatic. And... ruthless." He looked back at Leo, his eyes filled with a mixture of fear and pleading. "I didn't want to do it. I swear. But I... I felt like I had no choice."

"You *always* have a choice, Mr. Dvorak," Leo said, his voice firm. "And now, you have a choice to make. You can cooperate with us, tell us everything you know about Albin Varga, about 'Balance Keeper,' about Adrian's murder... or you can face the consequences alone."

Dvorak hesitated, his internal struggle evident in his expression. The proud Leo, the master manipulator, was now a cornered animal, his carefully constructed world collapsing around him.

Finally, with a sigh of defeat, he nodded. "I'll... I'll tell you everything," he said, his voice barely a whisper. "But you need to understand... Albin Varga... he's not like anyone you've ever met. He's... dangerous. He's capable of anything."

Leo met his gaze, his expression unwavering. "We're prepared for that, Mr. Dvorak. We're prepared for *anything*." He knew this was just the beginning of the final confrontation, the unraveling of the *true* conspiracy. The unseen hand was about to be revealed.

Leo stood up.

"Take me to him." He said

Chapter 15

Dvorak's confession, his fear-filled admission of Albin Varga's involvement, had blown the case wide open. The carefully constructed puzzle they'd been piecing together had suddenly shattered, revealing a new, even more complex and disturbing picture. They had a name, a motive, and a direction – but they needed proof, and they needed to understand the full extent of Albin Varga's role.

Their first step was to learn everything they could about Adrian's uncle. They returned to Leo's office, the familiar clutter of files, photographs, and the corkboard offering a sense of grounding amidst the swirling uncertainty.

"We need to find out everything we can about Albin Varga," Leo said, his voice firm with resolve. "His research, his connections, his... motivations." He was already accessing databases, searching for any information on the elusive professor.

Maggie, meanwhile, focused on Adrian's files, searching for any mention of his uncle, any hint of their relationship, any clue that might shed light on the current situation.

"Adrian and his uncle were close," Maggie said, her voice thoughtful, scanning through a series of emails. "They collaborated on several research projects, they attended conferences together... but there's something... strained in their communication. A subtle tension, a hint of disagreement."

Leo nodded, his own research yielding similar results. Albin Varga was a brilliant, but controversial figure, a theoretical physicist whose work on balance and equilibrium bordered on the esoteric. He was a Libra, a sign associated with harmony and justice, but Leo had learned that every sign had its shadow side, its potential for darkness.

"Look at this," Leo said, pointing to an article about Albin Varga. "He was involved in a... dispute with the university several years ago. Accusations of... unethical research practices. It was all very hush-hush, but it suggests a... willingness to bend the rules, to push the boundaries."

"And Adrian... he was a Gemini," Maggie added, her brow furrowed in thought. "Curious, inquisitive, always seeking knowledge, always questioning... He might have stumbled onto something he shouldn't have. Something related to his uncle's research."

"Something that threatened Albin Varga's work, his reputation... or something even bigger," Leo finished, his voice grim. He considered the possibilities, the potential for groundbreaking discoveries, for dangerous technologies, for secrets that someone was willing to kill to protect.

They spent hours piecing together the fragments of information, building a profile of Albin Varga, a man who remained shrouded in mystery, a man who seemed to exist on the fringes of the scientific community, a man who might hold the key to unlocking the entire conspiracy.

As the night wore on, a sense of unease settled over them. They were dealing with forces they didn't fully understand, with a potential mastermind who was far more dangerous than Dvorak or Novotny.

"We need to find him, Maggie," Leo said, his voice filled with a sense of urgency. "We need to find Albin Varga and find out what he knows."

But finding Albin Varga proved to be more difficult than they anticipated. He had no fixed address, no listed phone number, no obvious online presence. He seemed to have vanished, disappearing into the shadows, leaving behind only a trail of unanswered questions and a growing sense of dread.

"He's a ghost," Maggie said, her voice filled with frustration. "It's like he doesn't even exist."

"He exists," Leo replied, his voice firm with resolve. "And we'll find him. We have to." He knew they were running out of time, that the scales of justice were tipping precariously, and that the final confrontation was rapidly approaching. They were close to exposing the hidden mastermind, but they were also closer than ever to the darkness that lay at the heart of the conspiracy.

"He is a Libra, maybe we can review their patronages" Leo said.

"Good idea" Maggie said.

They prepared themselfs.

THE QUEST TO LOCATE Albin Varga consumed them. They knew he held the key to understanding the deeper conspiracy, the "forces" that had led to Adrian's murder. But Varga was a ghost, a phantom with no readily available digital footprint.

Their initial efforts yielded nothing. No current address, no phone number, no recent publications. It was as if he had deliberately erased himself from the public record. Leo, however, remembered something from Varga's file – *Libra*. He decided to approach the problem from a different angle.

"Libras value relationships, connections, harmony," Leo mused, tapping a finger on the corkboard, his gaze fixed on the few scraps of information they had about Varga. "They're unlikely to be complete loners. There has to be *someone* who knows where he is, someone he trusts."

Maggie nodded, understanding his line of reasoning. "So, we focus on his known associates? Colleagues, friends, family... anyone who might have a connection to him."

They began to meticulously reconstruct Albin Varga's network, using the limited information they had gleaned from Adrian's files, from online databases, and from Maggie's journalistic contacts. They focused on individuals who had co-authored papers with Varga, who had attended the same conferences, who had shared any kind of professional or personal connection.

It was a slow, painstaking process, filled with dead ends and frustrating silences. But Leo, driven by his intuition and his understanding of human behavior, refused to give up. He knew that somewhere, in the intricate web of relationships surrounding Albin Varga, there was a thread that would lead them to the truth.

After hours of searching, a name surfaced that sparked Leo's interest: Dr. Milena Horáková, a former colleague of Varga's at Charles University. Her name had appeared several times in connection with Varga's research, and she was listed as a co-author on several of his earlier publications.

"A Virgo," Leo murmured, noting Dr. Horáková's birthdate. "Detail-oriented, analytical, practical... and possibly harboring a sense of guilt or responsibility if she knows something about Varga's current activities."

Maggie quickly located Dr. Horáková's contact information – a university email address and a phone number. They decided to approach her cautiously, not revealing the full extent of their investigation, but hinting at their interest in Albin Varga's research.

Maggie sent an email, carefully crafted to pique Dr. Horáková's interest without raising suspicion. She posed as a journalist writing an article about prominent Czech scientists, expressing a particular interest in Varga's groundbreaking work on balance and equilibrium.

The response was surprisingly prompt. Dr. Horáková agreed to meet with them, suggesting a café near the university campus.

As they waited for Dr. Horáková, Leo and Maggie reviewed their strategy. They needed to be careful, observant, and sensitive to any cues that might reveal more than the woman was willing to say directly.

Dr. Horáková arrived precisely on time, a woman in her late fifties, with a sharp, intelligent gaze and a demeanor that suggested both curiosity and caution. She was, as Leo had predicted, a Virgo – meticulous, analytical, and guarded.

They exchanged pleasantries, Maggie leading the conversation with carefully phrased questions about Dr. Horáková's work and her past collaboration with Albin Varga.

"Professor Varga was a brilliant man," Dr. Horáková said, her voice measured, her eyes betraying a hint of... sadness? Regret? "But also... unconventional. He had... strong beliefs. About the nature of reality, about the potential of science... and about the dangers of unchecked ambition."

"Dangers?" Leo asked, gently probing.

Dr. Horáková hesitated, then sighed. "He believed that some forces... some knowledge... should remain hidden. That some doors are best left unopened."

"And Adrian... did he share those beliefs?" Maggie asked, her voice low and intense.

Dr. Horáková looked down at her hands, her expression troubled. "Adrian was... different. He was... driven. He wanted to... push the boundaries. He wanted to... prove his uncle wrong."

"And did he?" Leo asked, his gaze fixed on Dr. Horáková's face.

Dr. Horáková looked up, her eyes meeting Leo's, a flicker of fear in their depths. "I... I don't know," she whispered. "But I fear... he may have stumbled onto something... something dangerous. Something that... someone... wanted to keep secret."

"Someone like... Albin Varga?" Maggie pressed, her voice barely audible.

Dr. Horáková didn't answer directly. Instead, she reached into her bag and pulled out a small, folded piece of paper. "I haven't seen Albin in years," she said, her voice trembling slightly. "But... he sent me this. A few weeks ago. I... I didn't know what to make of it. Perhaps... perhaps you can."

She handed the paper to Leo. It was a short, cryptic message, written in a shaky hand: *The scales are tipping. The balance must be restored. Tell no one.* And below, a single initial: *A*.

Leo and Maggie exchanged a look of profound understanding. The message confirmed their suspicions, solidified their belief that Albin Varga was the key to unlocking the entire conspiracy. But it also raised more questions. What did Varga mean by "the scales are tipping"? What balance was he trying to restore? And who was he warning Dr. Horáková *not* to tell?

Maggie looked to Leo.

Leo stood up "We need to find him, and maybe, save him"

ARMED WITH DR. HORÁKOVÁ'S cryptic message and the growing suspicion that Albin Varga was the key to the entire conspiracy, Leo and Maggie knew they needed to shift their focus. Dvorak had admitted to orchestrating the sabotage, but under duress, claiming Albin Varga was the true mastermind. Novotny was still a suspect, but his cryptic remarks about "forces" and his refusal to speak further without a lawyer suggested a deeper, more complex game afoot.

Before confronting Varga – *if* they could find him – they decided to revisit Novotny. They needed to test his reactions, to see if his fear, his carefully constructed Capricorn defenses, would crack under the weight of the new evidence pointing towards Albin Varga.

The sleek, modern interior of Novotny Solutions felt less like a place of business and more like a carefully constructed stage for a deadly drama. When they were ushered into Novotny's office, the man greeted them with his usual polished smile, but Leo, attuned to the subtle cues of human behavior, detected a flicker of apprehension in his eyes, a subtle tension in his posture.

"Detective Maxwell, Ms. Hart," Novotny said, his voice smooth and controlled, gesturing for them to sit. "This is becoming a regular occurrence. Have you made any progress in your... investigation?"

Leo ignored the veiled sarcasm, his gaze fixed on Novotny's face. "We have," he replied, his voice low and steady. "We've uncovered new evidence. Evidence that suggests... you weren't entirely truthful with us."

Novotny's smile faltered, a brief, almost imperceptible crack in his Capricorn façade. "I'm not sure what you mean."

Maggie leaned forward, her voice sharp, cutting through the pretense. "We know about 'Project Oversight,' Mr. Novotny. We know about the emails, the financial transactions, the recording. And we know that you weren't working alone."

Novotny's jaw tightened, a subtle but telling sign of his internal struggle. "I've already told you everything I know."

"You told us you wouldn't harm Adrian," Leo countered, his voice unwavering. "You told us you had nothing to do with his death. But the evidence suggests otherwise. And your own words... 'forces he didn't understand'... suggest there's more to this story than you've revealed."

They pressed him, not with accusations, but with questions, with carefully worded statements designed to probe his defenses, to expose the cracks in his carefully constructed façade. Leo watched him closely, observing his reactions, his body language, his tone of voice – the subtle cues that betrayed the truth.

"Who were you communicating with, Mr. Novotny?" Maggie asked, her voice gentle but persistent. "Who was 'Project Oversight'?"

Novotny hesitated, his eyes darting between Leo and Maggie, his Capricorn pragmatism warring with his fear. He was trapped, caught in a web of his own making, and he knew it.

"I... I can't," he stammered, his voice barely a whisper. "I can't tell you."

"Is it Dvorak?" Leo pressed, his voice low and intense. "Is he the one pulling the strings?"

Novotny shook his head, his eyes filled with a mixture of fear and... something else. Was it regret? Guilt? Or something far more complex?

"It's... it's bigger than Dvorak," he finally said, his voice barely audible. "It's... something else. Something... dangerous."

"Something related to Albin Varga's research?" Maggie asked, her voice sharp with intuition.

Novotny's reaction was immediate and visceral. His face paled, his eyes widened in shock and terror. He opened his mouth to speak, but no words came out. He looked like a man who had just seen a ghost.

"Albin Varga," Leo repeated, his voice firm and unwavering. "What is his role in all of this, Mr. Novotny? What is 'Balance Keeper' *really* about?"

Novotny's carefully constructed defenses crumbled. He looked from Leo to Maggie, his eyes filled with a desperate, pleading fear. "I... I can't tell you," he whispered. "He'll... they'll..." He stopped, unable to continue, his body trembling visibly.

"They'll *what*, Mr. Novotny?" Leo pressed, his voice relentless. "Kill you? Like they killed Adrian?"

Novotny closed his eyes, his body slumping in defeat. He was a broken man, a Capricorn whose carefully constructed world had collapsed around him. He knew he was trapped, caught between his fear of Leo and Maggie and his even greater fear of... something else. Something far more powerful, far more dangerous.

"I... I can't," he repeated, his voice barely a whisper. "I just... can't."

Leo and Maggie exchanged a look of grim understanding. They had reached another impasse, another wall of silence. But they had also confirmed their suspicions. Albin Varga was the key. He was the hidden mastermind, the puppet master pulling the strings. And he was far more dangerous than they had ever imagined.

Leo stood up, his expression resolute. "We'll find him, Mr. Novotny," he said, his voice cold and hard. "And when we do, we'll uncover the *full* truth. No matter how dark, no matter how dangerous."

He look at Maggie.

And said.

"Let's go"

Chapter 16

Novotny's terror, his stark refusal to name Albin Varga, had confirmed their suspicions: they were dealing with a force far more powerful and dangerous than they had initially imagined. The carefully constructed puzzle of corporate espionage and personal vendettas had shattered, revealing a deeper, more unsettling conspiracy.

They needed to find Albin Varga, and they needed to do it quickly. But Varga was a ghost, a phantom with no readily available digital footprint, no obvious connections. They were starting from scratch, with only a name, a profession, and a cryptic message from a terrified man.

"We know he's a Libra," Leo said, his voice thoughtful, pacing his cluttered office. "We know he's a theoretical physicist, specializing in balance and equilibrium. And we know he was close to Adrian, at least at one point." He stopped pacing, his gaze settling on the corkboard, on the photograph of Adrian and his uncle. "We need to understand their relationship, Maggie. We need to find out what happened between them."

Maggie nodded, her mind already racing, considering the possibilities. "We should start with Adrian's files," she said. "See if there's any mention of his uncle, any correspondence, any hint of their collaboration... or their conflict."

They spent hours poring over Adrian's digital archive, searching for any trace of Albin Varga. They found references to his research, mentions of his name in academic papers, but nothing that shed light on their personal relationship, nothing that explained Adrian's fear, Novotny's terror, or Dvorak's desperate attempt to conceal the truth.

It was Maggie who made the first breakthrough. While examining Adrian's personal emails, she discovered a series of messages exchanged with a Dr. Milena Horáková – the Virgo colleague of Albin Varga's they had briefly encountered before.

"Look at this," Maggie said, her voice filled with a mixture of excitement and apprehension. "Adrian was confiding in Dr. Horáková. He was... worried. About his uncle. About his research. About something he called 'the instability.'"

Leo leaned closer, his eyes scanning the emails. The messages were cryptic, filled with veiled references and ambiguous warnings. But one phrase stood out: *"He's not who you think he is, Milena. He's capable of anything."*

"He's talking about his uncle," Leo murmured, his voice grim. "Adrian was afraid of Albin Varga."

"But *why*?" Maggie asked, her brow furrowed in thought. "What was he afraid of?"

They delved deeper into the emails, piecing together the fragments of information, trying to decipher Adrian's cryptic warnings. They discovered that Adrian had become increasingly concerned about his uncle's research, about the potential consequences of his discoveries, about the forces he might be unleashing.

"The instability," Leo repeated, his voice thoughtful. "What did he mean by that?" He considered the possibilities, the implications of Albin Varga's work on balance and equilibrium. Could it be a metaphor? Or something... literal?

"We need to talk to Dr. Horáková again," Maggie said, her voice firm with resolve. "She might know more than she's letting on. She might be able to help us understand what Adrian was afraid of."

They decided to approach Dr. Horáková cautiously, not revealing the full extent of their knowledge, but seeking clarification, seeking answers to the questions that were swirling in their minds.

As night descended upon Prague, casting long shadows across the city, Leo and Maggie prepared for their next encounter, their next step in the unraveling of the conspiracy. They knew they were close to the truth, but they also knew that the truth might be far more dangerous than they had ever imagined. The silent witness had spoken, his cryptic message echoing in their minds, and they were determined to follow his words, to uncover the hidden mastermind, to finally bring justice to Adrian and to all those who had been caught in the web of deceit.

They were ready.

THEIR PLAN WAS SET: a cautious, indirect approach to Dr. Milena Horáková, seeking answers without revealing the full extent of their investigation. They needed to understand the nature of Albin Varga's research, his relationship with Adrian, and the potential connection to "Balance Keeper" and the murder.

Maggie's carefully worded email, posing as a journalist researching prominent Czech scientists, had yielded a surprisingly prompt response. Dr. Horáková had agreed to meet them at a café near Charles University, a location that felt both familiar and fraught with a new layer of uncertainty.

As they waited for Dr. Horáková, Leo and Maggie reviewed their strategy. They needed to be observant, sensitive to any cues, any hesitation, any flicker of fear or guilt that might betray a deeper knowledge.

Dr. Horáková arrived precisely on time, a woman in her late fifties, with a sharp, intelligent gaze and a demeanor that suggested both curiosity and a carefully guarded reserve. *Virgo*, Leo thought, noting her meticulous appearance, her precise movements. He knew they would need to be patient, to earn her trust, to draw out the information they needed.

They exchanged pleasantries, Maggie leading the conversation with carefully phrased questions about Dr. Horáková's work and her past collaboration with Albin Varga.

"Professor Varga was a brilliant man," Dr. Horáková said, her voice measured, her eyes betraying a hint of... sadness? Regret? Perhaps a complex mixture of both. "But also... unconventional. He had... strong beliefs. About the nature of reality, about the potential of science... and about the dangers of unchecked ambition."

"Dangers?" Leo asked, gently probing, his voice calm and reassuring.

Dr. Horáková hesitated, then sighed, a subtle release of tension. "He believed that some forces... some knowledge...

should remain hidden. That some doors are best left unopened."

"And Adrian... did he share those beliefs?" Maggie asked, her voice low and intense, her gaze fixed on Dr. Horáková's face.

Dr. Horáková looked down at her hands, her expression troubled. "Adrian was... different. He was... driven. He was a Gemini, always searching. He wanted to... push the boundaries. He wanted to... prove his uncle wrong." A flicker of something unreadable crossed her face – perhaps a hint of admiration, perhaps a trace of fear.

"And did he?" Leo asked, his voice soft but insistent.

Dr. Horáková looked up, her eyes meeting Leo's, a flicker of fear in their depths. "I... I don't know," she whispered. "But I fear... he may have stumbled onto something... something dangerous. Something that... someone... wanted to keep secret."

"Someone like... his uncle?" Maggie pressed, her voice barely audible.

Dr. Horáková didn't answer directly. Instead, she reached into her bag and pulled out a small, folded piece of paper. "I haven't seen Albin in years," she said, her voice trembling slightly. "But... he sent me this. A few weeks ago. I... I didn't know what to make of it. Perhaps... perhaps you can."

She handed the paper to Leo. It was a short, cryptic message, written in a shaky hand: *The scales are tipping. The balance must be restored. Tell no one.* And below, a single initial: *A.*

Leo and Maggie exchanged a look of profound understanding. The message confirmed their suspicions, solidified their belief that Albin Varga was the key to unlocking the entire conspiracy. But it also raised more questions. What did Varga mean by "the scales are tipping"? What balance was he trying to restore? And who was he warning Dr. Horáková *not* to tell? This fragile alliance, born of shared concern and a flicker of trust, had yielded a crucial piece of the puzzle.

Leo carefully refolded the note, his mind racing. "Dr. Horáková," he said, his voice serious but gentle, "do you know where we can find Albin Varga?"

Dr. Horáková shook her head, her eyes filled with a mixture of fear and helplessness. "I don't," she whispered. "I haven't seen him in years. After... after the incident at the university... he withdrew. He became... reclusive."

"The incident?" Leo prompted, his gaze unwavering.

Dr. Horáková hesitated, then took a deep breath. "There were... accusations," she said, her voice barely audible. "Unethical research practices. Experiments that... crossed the line. It was all very... hush-hush. But Albin... he was forced to resign. He lost everything."

"And you believe this is connected to Adrian's death?" Maggie asked, her voice low and intense.

Dr. Horáková nodded slowly. "I... I don't know for sure," she said. "But... I fear it is. Albin... he was obsessed with his work. With balance. With... control. And Adrian... he was getting too close. He was asking too many questions." She looked at Leo and Maggie, her eyes pleading. "Please," she whispered. "Be careful. Albin... he's not... he's not himself anymore."

The weight of her words, the unspoken warning, settled heavily upon them. They had a name, a motive, and a cryptic message. But they still didn't know where Albin Varga was, or what he was planning. They were chasing a ghost, a shadow, a man driven by a dangerous obsession and a desperate need to restore a balance that only he seemed to understand.

"Do you know were can we start looking?" Leo asked.

Dr. Horáková thought for a moment, and whisper "His old house."

DR. HORÁKOVÁ'S WARNING – "He's not himself anymore" – echoed in Leo's mind as he and Maggie prepared for their next move. They had a name, a motive, a cryptic message, and a possible location: Albin Varga's old house. But they also had a growing sense of unease, a feeling that they were dealing with something far more complex and dangerous than they had initially anticipated.

Before seeking out Varga, however, they decided to make one final attempt to extract information from Dvorak. They knew he was withholding crucial details, that he was afraid, and that he held a key piece of the puzzle.

The opulent office of Dvorak Technologies felt colder, more menacing than before. Dvorak himself seemed diminished, his usual leonine confidence replaced by a nervous energy, his eyes darting around the room as if expecting danger to materialize at any moment.

"Mr. Dvorak," Leo began, his voice calm but firm, "we know about Albin Varga. We know about his involvement in 'Balance Keeper.' And we know about your... collaboration with him."

Dvorak's carefully constructed façade crumbled. He sagged in his chair, his gaze fixed on the floor, his body language radiating defeat. The proud Leo, accustomed to controlling every situation, was now a broken man.

"I... I told you," he whispered, his voice barely audible. "I didn't want to do it. I had no choice."

"You *always* have a choice, Mr. Dvorak," Maggie said, her voice softer now, but still firm. "And now, you have a choice to make. Cooperate with us, tell us everything you know, or face the consequences alone."

Dvorak looked up, his eyes filled with a mixture of fear and desperation. "He... he'll kill me," he whispered. "If I talk... he'll kill me."

"Who, Mr. Dvorak?" Leo pressed, his voice gentle but insistent. "Albin Varga?"

Dvorak nodded slowly, his body trembling. "He's... he's not the man he used to be. He's... obsessed. With his research... with the balance... with... power." He paused, his gaze shifting to the window, as if seeing something beyond the cityscape. "He said... he said Adrian was a threat. That he was going to... expose everything. That he was going to... disrupt the balance."

"What balance, Mr. Dvorak?" Maggie asked, her voice sharp with urgency. "What is 'Balance Keeper' *really* about?"

Dvorak hesitated, his internal struggle evident in his expression. He looked at Leo, then at Maggie, his eyes pleading for understanding, for help.

"It's... it's about his research," he finally said, his voice barely a whisper. "About... harnessing energy. About... controlling forces that... that shouldn't be controlled." He shook his head, his eyes filled with a growing terror. "It's... it's madness. It's... dangerous."

"And Adrian... he discovered this?" Leo asked, his voice low and intense.

Dvorak nodded. "He... he found out what Albin was really doing. He tried to... to stop him. He threatened to... to go public."

"And that's why Albin Varga had him killed?" Maggie pressed, her voice filled with a mixture of disbelief and horror.

Dvorak looked at them, his eyes filled with a chilling certainty. "Albin... he doesn't see it as murder," he said, his voice barely audible. "He sees it as... restoring balance. As... eliminating a threat to his... grand design."

"And Novotny?" Leo asked. "Where does he fit into all of this?"

"Novotny... he was just a... a facilitator," Dvorak said, his voice dismissive. "A tool. He provided the... resources. The technology. The... connections. He was useful... until he wasn't."

"And you, Mr. Dvorak?" Maggie asked, her voice soft but unwavering. "What was your role?"

Dvorak looked down at his hands, his expression a mixture of shame and regret. "I... I was blinded by ambition," he whispered. "By the promise of... power. Of... recognition. I didn't see... I didn't *want* to see... the darkness behind Albin's brilliance. I was a fool."

Leo and Maggie exchanged a look of grim understanding. They had finally uncovered the truth, or at least, a significant portion of it. Albin Varga was the mastermind, the driving force behind the conspiracy. Dvorak was a pawn, a willing participant, but ultimately, a victim of his own ambition and Varga's manipulative power. Now, they are going for him.

Leo stood.

"Where can find him?"

Dvorak look at him, and point his finger to a draw.

Leo went, and took a paper.

"This is it," said Dvorak

Leo look at the paper, turn to Maggie

"It's time"

Chapter 17

Dvorak's confession had confirmed their suspicions, but it had also opened a Pandora's Box of new questions. Albin Varga, the elusive uncle, the brilliant and potentially dangerous physicist, was now their primary focus. They needed to find him, to understand his motives, to uncover the full extent of his involvement in Adrian's murder and the chilling "Balance Keeper" project.

They decided to start by tracking down the address Dvorak had provided – Albin Varga's old house. It was a long shot, a gamble, but they had little else to go on. Varga was a ghost, a phantom with no readily available digital footprint, no obvious connections beyond his estranged colleague, Dr. Horáková, and his now-deceased nephew.

The house was located in a quiet, secluded neighborhood on the outskirts of Prague, a far cry from the bustling city center where they had spent so much of their time. It was an old, rambling structure, with a neglected garden and an air of faded grandeur. The windows were dark, the curtains drawn, and a thick layer of dust covered the doorstep. It looked... abandoned.

Leo approached the front door cautiously, his hand hovering near his holster, his senses on high alert. He was acutely aware that they were stepping into the unknown, confronting a potentially dangerous and unpredictable individual. He rang the doorbell, the sound echoing through the silent house.

No response.

He tried the doorknob, expecting it to be locked, but to his surprise, it turned. The door creaked open, revealing a dark, musty interior.

"Hello?" Leo called out, his voice echoing through the stillness. "Albin Varga? Police!"

Still no response.

Leo exchanged a look with Maggie, his expression grim. He drew his weapon, a precautionary measure, and stepped inside, Maggie close behind him.

The house was eerily silent, filled with the scent of dust and decay. The furniture was covered in white sheets, the air thick with a sense of abandonment. It was as if time had stopped, as if the occupants had simply vanished, leaving everything behind.

They moved through the house slowly, cautiously, their senses on high alert. They checked each room, each closet, each dark corner, searching for any sign of life, any clue that might shed light on Albin Varga's whereabouts, on his plans, on his motives.

The house, however, remained stubbornly silent, revealing nothing. It was a shell, a husk, a place devoid of life and warmth. It was a dead end.

Frustration began to mount. They had hoped to find Varga, to confront him, to get answers. But the house offered only

JUSTICE IN THE SHADOWS

silence, only shadows, only the lingering scent of a life that had once been.

It was in the study, a large, book-lined room with a dusty desk and a single, bare lightbulb hanging from the ceiling, that they found something. Not a person, not a clue to Varga's whereabouts, but a... presence.

The walls were covered in diagrams, equations, and symbols, a chaotic tapestry of scientific and esoteric markings. It was the workspace of a brilliant, obsessive mind, a mind consumed by a singular, all-encompassing pursuit.

Leo, with his understanding of human behavior and his subtle appreciation for the Zodiac, recognized the underlying pattern, the hidden order within the chaos. *Libra*. The sign of balance, of harmony, of justice... but also, potentially, of obsession, of fanaticism, of a distorted sense of equilibrium.

"This is it," Leo murmured, his voice filled with a mixture of awe and apprehension. "This is where he worked. This is where he... conceived his plans."

Maggie, meanwhile, was examining a large, leather-bound notebook that lay open on the desk. The pages were filled with Albin Varga's handwriting, a dense, intricate script that seemed to vibrate with an almost palpable energy.

"Look at this," Maggie said, her voice hushed, her eyes wide with a mixture of fascination and fear. "It's... it's a journal. His thoughts, his theories, his... experiments."

She began to read aloud, her voice trembling slightly as she deciphered Varga's words:

"The balance must be restored. The scales have tipped too far. The forces of chaos are threatening to overwhelm the forces of order. I must... I

Leo and Maggie exchanged a look of profound understanding. Varga's words confirmed their worst fears. He was not just a brilliant scientist; he was a fanatic, a zealot, driven by a distorted sense of justice, by a desperate need to impose his own twisted vision of balance upon the world.

"He's not just dangerous, Maggie," Leo said, his voice grim. "He's... delusional. He believes he's acting for the greater good, that he's... restoring order. But his methods... his actions... they're monstrous."

They continued to examine the journal, discovering more disturbing details about Varga's research, about his obsession with "harnessing zero-point energy," about his belief in a "unified field theory" that would allow him to control the very fabric of reality.

"This is... insane," Maggie whispered, her voice filled with a mixture of horror and disbelief. "This is... science fiction. It's... impossible."

"Perhaps," Leo replied, his voice thoughtful. "Or perhaps... it's just beyond our current understanding. Perhaps Adrian... stumbled onto something real. Something that Albin Varga was willing to kill to protect."

They knew they were running out of time. Albin Varga was out there, somewhere, planning his next move, driven by his twisted vision of balance. And they were the only ones who could stop him. They had found his lair, his workspace, his... confession. But they still hadn't found *him*.

As they prepared to leave the house, Leo noticed something on the desk, a small, almost insignificant detail that he had previously overlooked. A photograph, face down, partially hidden beneath a stack of papers.

He picked it up, his heart pounding in his chest. It was a photograph of Albin Varga, standing next to... *Novotny*. They were both smiling, their arms around each other's shoulders, like old friends, like... collaborators.

Leo felt a chill run down his spine. The unseen hand, the hidden mastermind, had finally been revealed. But it wasn't who they expected. It was... *both* of them. A partnership, a twisted alliance, forged in a shared obsession, in a shared belief in a dangerous, distorted vision of balance.

Leo, showed the picture.

"We need to get to him, Now" Leo said

Maggie, with a new energy, said.

"Lets Go"

The photograph of Albin Varga and Gregor Novotny, smiling together like old friends, had shattered their previous assumptions. The conspiracy was more complex, more deeply rooted, than they had imagined. They now faced a formidable alliance, a partnership forged in a shared obsession and a willingness to commit unspeakable acts to protect their secrets.

Their immediate priority was to locate Albin Varga. Dr. Horáková had provided a starting point – his old house – but they knew it was a long shot. Varga was a recluse, a man who had deliberately withdrawn from society, a man who was likely to be cautious and well-prepared for any intrusion.

Before heading to the house, however, Leo decided to revisit the information they had gathered about Varga, seeking any clue, any detail, that might help them anticipate his actions, his mindset, his potential hiding places.

"He's a Libra," Leo mused, his gaze fixed on the photograph of Varga and Novotny, his mind sifting through the characteristics associated with the sign. "Balance, harmony, justice... those are the ideals. But every sign has its shadow side. Obsession, fanaticism, a distorted sense of... equilibrium."

Maggie nodded, her expression thoughtful. "And Novotny... he's the Capricorn. The pragmatist, the strategist, the one who values control and efficiency. It's a... dangerous combination."

"They complement each other," Leo agreed, his voice grim. "Varga's obsession, his intellectual brilliance, fueled by Novotny's resources, his connections, his... ruthlessness." He considered the implications, the potential for a conspiracy that reached far beyond corporate espionage, that delved into the realm of dangerous scientific research, of unchecked ambition, of a distorted vision of the future.

They spent hours poring over Varga's research papers, his academic publications, his personal notes, searching for any hint of his current whereabouts, any clue to his plans. They discovered a pattern of increasingly erratic behavior, a growing obsession with "restoring balance," a disturbing fascination with the power of "zero-point energy."

"This is... unsettling," Maggie said, her voice hushed, her eyes wide with a mixture of apprehension and disbelief. "He's talking about harnessing energy on a scale that... that could be catastrophic."

"He believes he's on the verge of a breakthrough," Leo said, his voice grim. "A discovery that will change everything. That will... restore balance to the world, according to his own twisted definition."

"And Adrian... he threatened to expose him," Maggie added, her voice barely a whisper. "He threatened to disrupt his plans."

"And that's why he had to be silenced," Leo finished, his voice filled with a chilling certainty.

They knew they were running out of time. Albin Varga was out there, somewhere, pursuing his dangerous research, driven by his obsession, and they were the only ones who could stop him. But first, they needed to find him.

As dusk settled over Prague, casting long shadows across the city, Leo and Maggie prepared to leave for Varga's old house. They knew it was a long shot, that Varga was unlikely to be there, but they had to start somewhere. They had to follow every lead, no matter how faint, how unlikely.

Leo checked his weapon, a precautionary measure, his senses on high alert. He knew they were stepping into the unknown, confronting a potentially dangerous and unpredictable individual, a man driven by a distorted vision of justice and a desperate need to restore a balance that only he seemed to understand.

Maggie, check the address on the GPS.

Leo, started the car.

"We need to be ready for anything" Leo said.

The photograph – Albin Varga and Gregor Novotny, arms around each other's shoulders, smiling – had changed everything. It was no longer a question of *if* Novotny was involved, but *how deeply*. Leo and Maggie decided to confront him, not with accusations, but with the undeniable evidence of his connection to Varga.

The sleek, modern interior of Novotny Solutions felt colder, more menacing than ever before. As they were ushered into Novotny's office, Leo felt a surge of adrenaline, a sense of anticipation mixed with a growing unease.

Novotny greeted them with his usual polished smile, but behind the Capricorn's mask of control, Leo detected a flicker of fear, a subtle tension that hadn't been there before. The balance of power had shifted.

"Detective Maxwell, Ms. Hart," Novotny said, his voice smooth but strained, gesturing for them to sit. "I presume this isn't a social call."

Leo placed the photograph on Novotny's desk, face up. The image of Novotny and Varga, smiling and relaxed, a stark contrast to the grim reality of the situation.

Novotny's reaction was immediate and visceral. His smile vanished, his face paled, his eyes widening in shock and disbelief. He stared at the photograph as if it were a venomous snake, his body stiffening with a mixture of fear and... recognition.

"Where... where did you get this?" he stammered, his voice barely a whisper.

"It doesn't matter," Leo replied, his voice cold and hard. "What matters is that we know about your connection to Albin Varga. We know about 'Balance Keeper.' And we know about your involvement in Adrian's murder."

Novotny's carefully constructed façade crumbled. He looked like a man who had been cornered, trapped, his secrets exposed. The pragmatic Capricorn, always in control, was now visibly shaken.

"I... I..." he stammered, unable to form a coherent sentence.

JUSTICE IN THE SHADOWS

"You told us you didn't know what forces Adrian was playing with," Maggie said, her voice sharp and accusing. "But you *did* know, didn't you? You knew *exactly* what he was involved in. You knew about Albin Varga's research. You knew about the danger."

Novotny looked from Maggie to Leo, his eyes filled with a desperate, pleading fear. "I... I didn't have a choice," he whispered. "He... he made me do it."

"Who made you do it, Mr. Novotny?" Leo pressed, his voice relentless. "Albin Varga?"

Novotny nodded slowly, his body trembling. "He... he said it was necessary. That Adrian was... a threat. That he was going to... disrupt the balance."

"The balance?" Maggie asked, her voice filled with a mixture of disbelief and horror. "What balance? What is 'Balance Keeper' *really* about?"

Novotny hesitated, his internal struggle evident in his expression. He looked like a man torn between his fear of Leo and Maggie and his even greater fear of Albin Varga.

"It's... it's about his research," he finally said, his voice barely audible. "About... harnessing energy. About... controlling forces that... that should remain untouched." He shook his head, his eyes filled with a growing terror. "It's... it's madness. It's... dangerous. It's beyond anything you can imagine."

"And Adrian... he discovered this?" Leo asked, his voice low and intense.

Novotny nodded. "He... he found out what Albin was really doing. He tried to... to stop him. He threatened to... to expose everything."

"And that's why Albin Varga had him killed?" Maggie pressed, her voice filled with a chilling certainty.

Novotny looked at them, his eyes filled with a haunting mixture of fear, guilt, and resignation. "Albin... he doesn't see it as murder," he whispered. "He sees it as... restoring equilibrium. As... eliminating a threat to his... grand design."

"And Dvorak?" Leo asked. "Where does he fit into all of this?"

"Dvorak... he was just a... a tool," Novotny said, his voice dismissive. "A means to an end. Albin... he used him. He manipulated his ego, his ambition, his... greed."

The full extent of the conspiracy, the chilling reality of Albin Varga's power and influence, was finally becoming clear. They had uncovered the hidden mastermind, the puppet master pulling the strings, the man driven by a dangerous obsession and a twisted vision of balance.

"Where is he, Novotny?" Leo's voice was steel.

Novotny hesitated, fear warring with a flicker of... something else. Defiance? Resignation? Perhaps even a sliver of hope that he could still salvage something from the wreckage of his life.

Then in a low voice, almost a whisper.

"I don't know." he said.

Leo, felt a chill.

"We need to find out" Leo said.

Chapter 18

The weight of Novotny's fear, his cryptic allusions to "forces" beyond their comprehension, and the chilling photograph of him with Albin Varga, had transformed the case into something far more complex and sinister than they had initially imagined. They were no longer simply investigating a murder; they were confronting a conspiracy that reached into the realms of dangerous science and twisted ideology.

Their immediate priority was to locate Albin Varga, the elusive Libra, the potential mastermind behind the entire operation. Dvorak had provided the location of Varga's old house, and Dr. Horáková had confirmed it was a place he used to frequent.

"We need to approach this cautiously," Leo said, his voice low and serious, as they prepared to leave for Varga's house. "We don't know what we're dealing with. We don't know what Varga is capable of."

Maggie nodded, her expression grim. "He's a scientist, not a soldier," she said, trying to reassure herself as much as Leo. "He's unlikely to be... physically dangerous."

"He's obsessed," Leo countered, his gaze fixed on the photograph of Varga and Novotny. "He's driven by a distorted vision of balance, of justice. And he's willing to kill to protect his secrets, to achieve his goals. That makes him *extremely* dangerous." He thought of the Libra symbol, the scales, and how easily they could be tipped from harmony into chaos.

They drove to Varga's house in silence, the tension thick between them. The house, located in a secluded, almost forgotten neighborhood on the outskirts of Prague, was an old, rambling structure, with a neglected garden and an air of faded grandeur. It looked... abandoned.

As they approached the front door, Leo felt a prickling sensation on the back of his neck, a sense of unease, of being watched. He scanned the surroundings, his eyes searching for any sign of movement, any indication of danger.

He rang the doorbell, the sound echoing through the silent house. No response.

He tried the doorknob, expecting it to be locked, but to his surprise, it turned. The door creaked open, revealing a dark, musty interior.

"Hello?" Leo called out, his voice echoing through the stillness. "Albin Varga? Police!"

Still no response.

Leo exchanged a look with Maggie, his expression grim. He drew his weapon, a precautionary measure, and stepped inside, Maggie close behind him, her own hand resting on the small pistol she carried in her bag.

The house was eerily silent, filled with the scent of dust and decay. The furniture was covered in white sheets, the air thick with a sense of abandonment. It was as if time had stopped, as if the occupants had simply vanished, leaving everything behind.

They moved through the house slowly, cautiously, their senses on high alert. They checked each room, each closet, each dark corner, searching for any sign of life, any clue that might shed light on Albin Varga's whereabouts, on his plans, on his motives.

The house, however, remained stubbornly silent, revealing nothing. It was a shell, a husk, a place devoid of warmth and life. It seemed like another dead end.

It was in the study, a large, book-lined room with a dusty desk and a single, bare lightbulb hanging from the ceiling, that they found something. Not a person, not a clue to Varga's whereabouts, but a... *presence*. An echo of the man's obsession, his twisted vision, his dangerous brilliance.

The walls were covered in diagrams, equations, and symbols, a chaotic tapestry of scientific and esoteric markings. It was the workspace of a brilliant, obsessive mind, a mind consumed by a singular, all-encompassing pursuit.

Leo, with his understanding of human behavior, recognized the underlying pattern, the hidden order within the chaos. *Libra*. The sign of balance, of harmony, of justice... but also, potentially, of obsession, of fanaticism, of a distorted sense of equilibrium.

"This is where he worked," Leo murmured, his voice filled with a mixture of awe and apprehension. "This is where he... developed his theories. Where he... planned."

Maggie, meanwhile, was examining a large, leather-bound notebook that lay open on the desk. The pages were filled with Albin Varga's handwriting, a dense, intricate script that seemed to vibrate with an almost palpable energy.

"Look at this," Maggie said, her voice hushed, her eyes wide with a mixture of fascination and fear. "It's... it's his journal. His thoughts, his theories, his... experiments."

She began to read aloud, her voice trembling slightly as she deciphered Varga's words:

"The balance must be restored. The scales have tipped too far. The forces of chaos are threatening to overwhelm the forces of order. I must... I

Leo and Maggie exchanged a look of profound understanding. Varga's words confirmed their worst fears. He was not just a brilliant scientist; he was a fanatic, a zealot, driven by a distorted sense of justice, by a desperate need to impose his own twisted vision of balance upon the world.

"He's not just dangerous, Maggie," Leo said, his voice grim. "He's... delusional. He believes he's acting for the greater good, that he's... restoring order. But his methods... his actions... they're monstrous."

They continued to examine the journal, discovering more disturbing details about Varga's research, about his obsession with "harnessing zero-point energy," about his belief in a "unified field theory" that would allow him to control the very fabric of reality. His words spoke of a power beyond human comprehension, a power that he believed he could wield to reshape the world according to his own twisted vision.

"This is... madness," Maggie whispered, her voice filled with a mixture of horror and disbelief. "This is... beyond anything we could have imagined."

"Perhaps," Leo replied, his voice thoughtful. "Or perhaps... it's just beyond our current understanding. Perhaps Adrian...

stumbled onto something real. Something that Albin Varga was willing to kill to protect. Something that *we* need to stop."

As they were about to leave the study.

Leo stop.

"Wait" he said.

He had a flash.

He took Maggie's hand.

"Lets go back to the begining."

THE ABANDONED HOUSE of Albin Varga, filled with shadows and the unsettling remnants of a brilliant, obsessive mind, had confirmed their worst fears: they were dealing with a dangerous fanatic, a man driven by a distorted vision of balance and a willingness to commit murder to achieve his goals. But the discovery of the photograph, showing Varga and *Novotny* together, had also revealed a new layer of complexity to the conspiracy.

They needed to reassess their strategy, to consider the possibility that Novotny was not just a facilitator, but a *co-conspirator*, a willing participant in Varga's grand, and potentially catastrophic, plan.

"We need to go back to Novotny," Leo said, his voice firm with resolve, as they drove back to the city, the unsettling images from Varga's house still fresh in their minds. "We need to confront him with the photograph, with everything we've learned. We need to break him."

Maggie nodded, her expression grim. "But we need to be careful, Leo. Novotny is a Capricorn, he's not going to crack easily. And if he realizes we're onto Varga... he might warn him. He might... do something drastic."

"I know," Leo agreed, his hand tightening on the steering wheel. "We need to be strategic. We need to use his own personality against him. His need for control, his pragmatism, his... fear."

They spent the rest of the drive formulating a plan, carefully considering their approach, anticipating Novotny's reactions, preparing for every possible contingency. They knew this confrontation would be different, more dangerous, than anything they had faced before. They were no longer dealing with corporate rivals or hired assassins; they were dealing with a partnership fueled by obsession and a willingness to sacrifice everything to achieve their goals.

Back at Leo's office, they reviewed the evidence against Novotny, focusing on the photograph, on Varga's journal, on Dr. Horáková's warning, on Dvorak's confession. They needed to present a united front, to show Novotny that they knew the truth, that his carefully constructed façade was crumbling.

"We'll approach him separately," Leo said, his voice low and thoughtful. "Maggie, you go first. Use your journalistic skills, your ability to connect with people, to get him to open up. Then, I'll step in, with the evidence, with the... pressure."

Maggie nodded, her expression determined. "We'll break him, Leo," she said, her voice filled with a quiet confidence. "We'll get him to talk. And then... we'll find Varga."

They knew time was running out. The anonymous text messages, the cryptic warnings, the sense of impending danger... it all pointed to a climax, a final confrontation. They were determined to be ready, to face whatever came their way,

JUSTICE IN THE SHADOWS

to bring the perpetrators to justice and to prevent whatever catastrophic plan Albin Varga had set in motion. The scales of justice were tipping, and they were determined to restore the balance, even if it meant risking everything.

Maggie said, her expression determined. "We'll break them and then we can move"

"We need to be two steps ahead" Leo said.

Following their plan, Maggie arrived at Novotny Solutions alone, requesting a meeting with Gregor Novotny under the guise of a follow-up interview for her (fictitious) article on cybersecurity. Leo remained behind, monitoring their communications and ready to intervene if necessary. He trusted Maggie's instincts, her ability to connect with people, to draw them out, to sense their vulnerabilities.

The atmosphere in Novotny's office was tense, the air thick with unspoken suspicion. Novotny greeted Maggie with his usual polished smile, but it seemed strained, his Capricorn control faltering under the weight of the mounting evidence.

"Ms. Hart," he said, his voice carefully neutral. "I wasn't expecting to see you again so soon."

"I had a few... follow-up questions," Maggie replied, her tone casual but her gaze sharp and observant. "Regarding your... collaboration with Dvorak Technologies. And... other ventures."

Novotny's smile wavered, a flicker of apprehension in his eyes. "I believe I've been quite clear about my relationship with Mr. Dvorak. It's purely professional."

Maggie leaned forward, her voice softening slightly. "Mr. Novotny, we know about 'Balance Keeper.' We know about Adrian's sabotage. And we know about your... involvement."

She paused, letting her words sink in. "But we also sense... that there's more to the story. That you're... afraid."

Novotny's jaw tightened, a subtle but telling sign of his internal struggle. He looked away, his gaze fixed on the cityscape outside, his expression a mixture of defiance and... vulnerability.

"I'm not afraid of anything," he said, his voice barely a whisper.

"Are you sure about that, Mr. Novotny?" Maggie pressed, her voice gentle but persistent. "Are you sure you're not afraid of... Albin Varga?"

The name hung in the air, a silent accusation, a trigger that shattered Novotny's carefully constructed façade. His reaction was immediate and visceral. His face paled, his hands trembling slightly, his eyes widening in shock and terror.

"How... how do you know about him?" he stammered, his voice barely audible.

Maggie didn't answer directly. Instead, she placed the photograph on the desk – the image of Novotny and Varga, smiling together, their arms around each other's shoulders. A silent testament to their partnership, their shared secrets, their dangerous alliance.

Novotny stared at the photograph, his expression a mixture of horror and disbelief. He looked like a man who had been cornered, his defenses crumbling, his secrets exposed.

"He... he's not who you think he is," Novotny whispered, his voice filled with a desperate, pleading fear. "He's... dangerous. He's... obsessed."

"With balance?" Maggie asked, her voice low and intense. "With restoring equilibrium?"

Novotny nodded slowly, his body trembling. "He... he believes he's doing what's necessary. That he's... saving the world. But he's... he's lost control. He's... gone too far."

"And Adrian... he discovered this?" Maggie pressed, her voice sharp with urgency.

Novotny nodded again. "He... he found out about Albin's research. About... the instability. About the... potential consequences. He tried to... to warn people. He tried to... to stop him."

"And that's why Albin Varga had him killed?" Maggie asked, her voice filled with a chilling certainty.

Novotny looked at her, his eyes filled with a haunting mixture of fear, guilt, and resignation. "Albin... he sees things differently," he whispered. "He sees... threats... where others see... progress. He sees... imbalance... where others see... innovation." He paused, his voice barely audible. "He believes... he's acting for the greater good. But he's... he's a monster."

It was at that moment, as Novotny's confession hung heavy in the air, that Leo entered the office. He had heard enough.

"Mr. Novotny," Leo said, his voice cold and hard, his gaze fixed on the broken man before him. "You're under arrest."

Novotny didn't resist. He simply closed his eyes, his body slumping in defeat. He was a Capricorn, stripped of his control, his carefully constructed world collapsing around him. He was a man caught in a web of his own making, a pawn in a game far more dangerous than he had ever imagined.

As Leo cuffed him. Novotny spoke.

"Be careful with Albin, He is very inteligent, and his research is..."

Leo cut him.

"We will be, now, tell us, where is he?"
Novotny, with a low voice said
"He is at the old observatory"
Maggie and Leo, look at each other.

Chapter 19

Novotny's confession, his chilling revelation about Albin Varga's obsession and the dangerous nature of "Balance Keeper," had brought them to the threshold of the truth. But the mastermind himself, the elusive Libra, remained out of reach. They had an address – Varga's old observatory – and a warning from Dvorak: *"He's not like anyone you've ever met. He's... dangerous." *

Before confronting Varga, Leo and Maggie needed to gather their resources, to prepare themselves for a potentially deadly encounter. They knew they were dealing with a brilliant, but unstable, individual, a man driven by a distorted vision of balance and a willingness to commit murder to achieve his goals.

"We need to understand his research," Leo said, his voice thoughtful, pacing his cluttered office. "We need to know what he's capable of, what he's planning, what this 'instability' is that Adrian discovered."

Maggie nodded, her expression grim. "And we need to find out more about his relationship with Novotny," she added. "How deeply involved was Novotny? Was he a willing participant, or was he... manipulated, like Dvorak?"

They decided to split their efforts. Maggie would focus on researching Albin Varga's scientific work, delving into his publications, his theories, his experiments, searching for any clue that might shed light on his current activities and his ultimate goals. Leo, meanwhile, would revisit the evidence they had gathered against Novotny, searching for any hidden communication, any financial transaction, any detail that might reveal the full extent of his involvement with Varga.

Maggie, immersed in the complex world of theoretical physics, found herself struggling to comprehend the full scope of Varga's research. His work was dense, esoteric, filled with complex equations and abstract concepts that were far beyond her understanding. But she persisted, driven by a sense of urgency, by a determination to uncover the truth.

She discovered that Varga's research focused on the concept of "zero-point energy," a theoretical source of unlimited, clean energy that existed in the vacuum of space. He believed that this energy could be harnessed, controlled, and used to... "restore balance" to the world.

"This is... insane," Maggie murmured, her voice filled with a mixture of awe and apprehension. "He's talking about manipulating the very fabric of reality."

Leo, meanwhile, was meticulously examining the encrypted messages between Novotny and Varga, the financial records, the recordings, searching for any hidden meaning, any overlooked detail. He was using his understanding of Novotny's Capricorn personality – his pragmatism, his need for control, his meticulous planning – to decipher the coded language, to uncover the true nature of their partnership.

He discovered a series of increasingly frantic messages from Novotny to Varga, expressing concern about Adrian's investigation, about the potential exposure of their plans, about the "instability" that Adrian had uncovered.

"Novotny was afraid," Leo said, his voice grim. "He knew that Varga was dangerous, that he was playing with forces he didn't understand. But he was also... complicit. He provided the resources, the technology, the... cover."

"He was enabling him," Maggie added, her voice filled with a growing sense of horror. "He was feeding his obsession."

They were interrupted by a sudden, sharp ringing – Leo's phone. He glanced at the caller ID, his expression hardening. It was an unknown number.

He hesitated for a moment, then answered, his voice cautious. "Maxwell."

A distorted voice, electronically altered, spoke from the other end. *"The scales are tipping, Detective. Time is running out. Choose wisely... or face the consequences." *

The line went dead.

Leo and Maggie exchanged a look of grim understanding. The anonymous messages, the cryptic warnings, had taken on a new, more menacing tone. They were no longer just taunts; they were threats.

"Varga knows we're close," Leo said, his voice low and intense. "He knows we're onto him. And he's... warning us."

"Or challenging us," Maggie added, her voice firm with resolve. "He wants us to... choose. To... back down. Or to... face him."

Leo nodded, his expression determined. "We have a choice to make, Maggie," he said, his voice unwavering. "We can back down, walk away, and let Varga continue his dangerous work. Or... we can confront him. We can stop him. We can... restore the balance."

He looked at Maggie, his eyes filled with a mixture of apprehension and determination. "What's it going to be?"

Maggie met his gaze, her expression resolute. "We finish this, Leo," she said, her voice filled with a quiet strength. "We find Varga. And we stop him. No matter the cost."

They knew they had to be ready, it was time.

THE OLD OBSERVATORY, Albin Varga's last known location, loomed before them, a dark silhouette against the twilight sky. It was a relic of a bygone era, a place of scientific inquiry now shrouded in an aura of mystery and potential danger. Leo and Maggie approached cautiously, their senses on high alert, their every step measured and deliberate.

They had spent the day preparing, gathering information, formulating a plan. They had reviewed Varga's research, his journal entries, his cryptic message to Dr. Horáková. They had analyzed his personality, his motivations, his potential weaknesses. They knew they were dealing with a brilliant, but unstable, individual, a man driven by a dangerous obsession and a willingness to commit murder to protect his secrets.

"He's a Libra," Leo murmured, his voice low and thoughtful, as they approached the observatory's entrance. "He values balance, harmony, justice... but his perception of those concepts is... distorted. He's obsessed with restoring an equilibrium that only he understands."

JUSTICE IN THE SHADOWS

Maggie nodded, her expression grim. "And he's willing to sacrifice anything... anyone... to achieve his goals." She thought of Adrian, of Dvorak, of Novotny, all pawns in Varga's twisted game.

The observatory's entrance was unlocked, a heavy wooden door that creaked ominously as they pushed it open. The interior was dark, dusty, and filled with the scent of decay. It was a place of shadows, of forgotten instruments, of a past that seemed to cling to the very walls.

They moved slowly, cautiously, their flashlights illuminating the darkness, their footsteps echoing through the silence. They searched each room, each corridor, each dusty corner, searching for any sign of Albin Varga, any clue to his plans, any indication of his current state of mind.

The observatory was a maze of interconnected rooms, filled with obsolete telescopes, astronomical charts, and strange, unidentifiable devices. It was a place of both science and mystery, a place where the boundaries between reality and imagination seemed to blur.

It was in the main observation dome, beneath the vast, star-studded expanse of the night sky, that they found the first sign of recent activity. A single, high-powered telescope was pointed towards a specific constellation, its lens gleaming in the faint moonlight.

Leo approached the telescope cautiously, his hand hovering near his holster. He peered through the eyepiece, his breath catching in his throat. He saw... nothing. Just the vast, empty expanse of space.

"What is it?" Maggie asked, her voice hushed, her eyes scanning the darkness.

"I don't know," Leo replied, his voice troubled. "He's looking at... nothing. Or... something we can't see." He considered the possibilities, the implications of Varga's research, his obsession with "zero-point energy," his belief in a "unified field theory."

Maggie, meanwhile, was examining a nearby table, covered in notes, diagrams, and calculations. She recognized some of the symbols from Varga's journal, the cryptic language of his twisted vision of balance.

"Look at this," she said, her voice filled with a mixture of apprehension and understanding. "He's... he's trying to... harness the energy of the stars. He's trying to... manipulate the very fabric of reality."

Leo joined her, his eyes scanning the notes, his mind racing to comprehend the full scope of Varga's plan. It was madness, it was impossible, it was... terrifying.

"He's not just trying to restore balance, Maggie," Leo said, his voice grim. "He's trying to... become a god. He's trying to... control the universe."

They were interrupted by a sudden, sharp sound – a creaking floorboard, a rustling curtain, a whisper of movement in the darkness.

Leo and Maggie froze, their senses on high alert, their bodies tensed for action. They were not alone.

"Albin Varga?" Leo called out, his voice echoing through the dome. "We know you're here. We know what you've done. It's over."

A moment of silence, then a voice, cold and calm, answered from the shadows.

"Over?" the voice said, a hint of amusement in its tone. "It's only just begun."

Albin Varga stepped out of the darkness, his figure silhouetted against the faint glow of the moonlit sky. He was an older man, tall and gaunt, with piercing blue eyes that seemed to burn with an unnatural intensity. He was dressed in a simple, dark suit, his hands clasped behind his back, his posture radiating an air of calm authority, of unwavering conviction.

He was... the silent witness. And he was... ready to speak.

Leo and Maggie look at him, and got ready.

ALBIN VARGA STOOD BEFORE them, a silhouette against the vast, star-studded sky visible through the observatory dome, his voice a chillingly calm counterpoint to the chaos he had unleashed. He was older than Leo had imagined, but his eyes, even in the dim light, held a sharp, unsettling intensity. *Libra*, Leo thought, *but a Libra with the scales tipped irrevocably towards darkness.*

"You've been busy, Detective Maxwell, Ms. Hart," Varga said, his voice smooth, almost melodic, but with an underlying current of steel. "Following the threads, unraveling the web... I must say, I'm impressed."

"We know about 'Balance Keeper,' Mr. Varga," Leo replied, his voice firm, his gaze unwavering. "We know about Adrian, about Dvorak, about Novotny. We know about *you*."

Varga chuckled softly, a sound that sent a shiver down Maggie's spine. "You know *nothing*," he said. "You see the shadows, the surface ripples, but you don't comprehend the depths. You don't understand the... *necessity*."

"The necessity of murder?" Maggie challenged, her voice trembling slightly, but filled with righteous anger. "The necessity of manipulating and exploiting others to achieve your... *goals*?"

Varga turned his gaze towards Maggie, his eyes seeming to pierce through her, to assess her, to judge her. "You speak of justice, Ms. Hart? Of morality? Such... limited concepts. Such... *human* concerns."

"What other concerns are there?" Leo asked, his voice low and intense. "What is this 'balance' you're so obsessed with restoring?"

Varga smiled, a slow, chilling smile that revealed a hint of... madness. "The universe, Detective Maxwell, is a delicate ecosystem. A complex interplay of forces, of energies, of... possibilities. And it is... *out of balance*. Tilted towards chaos, towards entropy, towards... destruction."

"And you believe you can... fix that?" Maggie asked, her voice filled with disbelief. "With... your research?"

"I *know* I can," Varga replied, his voice filled with an unwavering conviction. "I have discovered the key. The... *secret*. The power to harness the very fabric of reality. To... reshape the world. To... restore the balance."

"By killing your own nephew?" Leo pressed, his voice hard. "By manipulating Dvorak and Novotny? By... by unleashing whatever this 'instability' is that Adrian discovered?"

Varga's smile faded, replaced by a look of cold, calculating anger. "Adrian was... a threat. A loose end. He was... *weak*. He couldn't comprehend the... grandeur of my vision. He was... an obstacle."

"He was your *family*," Maggie said, her voice choked with emotion.

Varga dismissed her words with a wave of his hand. "Sentimentality, Ms. Hart. A... human weakness. I am beyond such... trivial concerns. I am concerned with the... *greater good*. With the... *survival* of the universe itself."

"You're delusional," Leo said, his voice filled with disgust. "You're a murderer, driven by a twisted sense of... justice. By a... god complex."

Varga laughed again, a harsh, grating sound that echoed through the observatory dome. "Perhaps," he said. "But I am also... inevitable. You cannot stop me, Detective Maxwell. You cannot stop... the balance from being restored."

"We'll see about that," Leo replied, his hand moving towards his holster, his eyes locked on Varga's. He knew this was the final confrontation, the culmination of their investigation, the moment of truth.

Varga, noticed and said.

"I am unarmed, Detective, I pose no threat to you at this very moment"

Leo hesitated, not sure, if he should trust him.

Maggie, grab Leo's hand, making him understand.

"We can't, we need him alive"

Leo, took a deep breath and said

"We are taking you, now, you have the right to remain silent..."

Before Leo could finish.

Varga, extended his arm, and point it to Leo, a bright light came, and pushed Leo, against the wall.

Maggie, got scared, she scream.

"LEO"

Varga look at her.

"Now, now, let's not make this any harder"

Chapter 20

The confrontation with Albin Varga had been a terrifying revelation. He was not just a brilliant scientist with a distorted vision of balance; he was a powerful, potentially unstable individual capable of wielding forces they barely understood. Leo's injury, though not life-threatening, served as a stark reminder of the danger they faced.

As Leo recovered, Maggie took the lead, her journalistic instincts kicking in. They needed to understand Varga's research, his motivations, his *capabilities*. They needed to find a way to stop him, to prevent him from carrying out his catastrophic plan.

"We need to go back to his journal," Maggie said, her voice firm with resolve, as they sat in Leo's office, the remnants of their investigation scattered around them. "There has to be something there, some clue, some weakness, that we can exploit."

Leo nodded, his expression grim. He was still shaken by the encounter with Varga, by the sheer power the man seemed to possess, but he was also determined to see this through, to bring the perpetrators to justice and to prevent further harm.

They spent hours poring over Varga's journal, deciphering his cryptic notes, his complex equations, his unsettling pronouncements about "restoring balance" and "harnessing zero-point energy." It was a daunting task, filled with scientific jargon and esoteric concepts that were far beyond their understanding.

"He's talking about manipulating reality itself," Maggie said, her voice hushed, her eyes wide with a mixture of awe and apprehension. "He believes he can... control the fundamental forces of the universe."

"And he's not just talking about it," Leo added, his voice grim. "He's *doing* it. He's experimenting, he's... building something. Something that... that could be incredibly dangerous."

They discovered detailed diagrams of a device, a complex apparatus that Varga referred to as the "Equilibrium Engine." It was a machine designed to harness and manipulate zero-point energy, to create a... "resonance cascade," to... "realign the fundamental forces of the universe."

"This is... insane," Maggie whispered, her voice trembling slightly. "This is... beyond anything we could have imagined."

"It's beyond anything *anyone* could have imagined," Leo agreed, his voice heavy with a sense of foreboding. "Except for Albin Varga. And... apparently... Adrian."

They continued to delve deeper into Varga's journal, uncovering more disturbing details about his research, his obsession, his twisted vision of the future. They learned that he believed the universe was inherently unstable, that it was tilting towards chaos, towards destruction, and that he, and only he, could restore the balance, could save humanity from itself.

"He sees himself as a savior," Maggie said, her voice filled with disgust. "A messiah. A... god."

"And he's willing to sacrifice anyone... anything... to achieve his goals," Leo added, his voice cold and hard.

They knew they were running out of time. Varga was out there, somewhere, preparing to unleash his "Equilibrium Engine," to carry out his catastrophic plan. They needed to find him, to stop him, before it was too late.

They also, needed to know what Novotny and Dvorak know.

"We need to re-think, all the steps, did we miss something?" Maggie, said.

"Yes" Leo said, and grab his notebook.

Leo's suggestion to "go back to the beginning" resonated with Maggie. They had uncovered a complex conspiracy, a web of deceit and manipulation, but they still lacked a complete understanding of the events that had led to Adrian's murder. They needed to re-examine the initial stages of their investigation, to revisit the evidence, the witnesses, the crime scene itself, with fresh eyes and a new perspective.

Their first stop was Adrian's apartment, the place where it had all begun. The apartment had been released by the police, the forensic teams had long since departed, but the space still held an echo of the violence, of the betrayal, of the unanswered questions.

They moved through the apartment slowly, deliberately, their senses on high alert. They were searching not for physical clues, but for... something else. A feeling, an impression, a detail that might have been overlooked in the initial chaos.

"We focused on the technology," Leo said, his voice low and thoughtful, his gaze sweeping across the room. "On the encrypted files, the digital footprints, the corporate connections. But what about the... human element? What about Adrian's personal life? His relationships? His fears?"

Maggie nodded, understanding his line of reasoning. "We know he was worried about his uncle's research," she said. "He was confiding in Dr. Horáková. He was... afraid."

They began to search the apartment again, this time focusing on the personal belongings, the items that reflected Adrian's personality, his interests, his connections. They examined his books, his photographs, his journals, his letters, searching for any hint of his state of mind in the days leading up to his death.

It was Leo who made the discovery. While examining a bookshelf, he noticed a small, almost hidden compartment behind a row of technical manuals. Inside, he found a collection of old photographs, letters, and... a small, leather-bound diary.

"Maggie, look at this," he said, his voice filled with a mixture of excitement and apprehension.

The diary was Adrian's, a personal record of his thoughts, his feelings, his observations. The entries were sporadic, often cryptic, but they offered a glimpse into the mind of a man who was increasingly troubled, increasingly fearful.

As they read through the diary, a new picture of Adrian began to emerge. He was not just a brilliant scientist, a driven innovator; he was also a sensitive, vulnerable individual, struggling with a growing sense of unease, with a growing suspicion that his uncle's research was far more dangerous than he had initially believed.

"He was starting to doubt Albin," Maggie said, her voice hushed, her eyes scanning the handwritten entries. "He was questioning his motives, his methods, his... sanity."

"And he was right to do so," Leo added, his voice grim. "Albin Varga was not just a brilliant scientist; he was a fanatic, a zealot, driven by a twisted vision of balance and a willingness to sacrifice anything... anyone... to achieve his goals."

The diary also revealed a growing sense of isolation, of loneliness. Adrian had few close friends, few people he trusted. He felt increasingly trapped, caught between his loyalty to his uncle and his growing fear of the consequences of his research.

One entry, dated just days before his death, stood out:

*"I feel like I'm standing on the edge of a precipice, looking into an abyss. I don't know what to do, who to trust. I'm afraid... so afraid... that I've unleashed something I can't control. Something that will... destroy everything." *

Leo and Maggie exchanged a look of profound understanding. Adrian's words were a chilling premonition, a testament to his growing awareness of the danger he faced, of the forces he had unwittingly unleashed.

"He knew," Maggie whispered, her voice filled with a mixture of sadness and horror. "He knew he was in danger. He knew... he was going to die."

"But he didn't know who to turn to," Leo added, his voice filled with a sense of frustration and regret. "He was alone. Isolated. Trapped."

The diary also contained a cryptic reference to a "safe place," a location where Adrian had hidden something of importance, something that he believed could expose the truth about his uncle's research, about "Balance Keeper," about the entire conspiracy.

"A safe place," Leo murmured, his mind racing. "Where? What did he mean?"

They searched the apartment again, this time with a new focus, a new determination. They looked for any clue, any hint, that might reveal the location of Adrian's "safe place."

As Leo, was about to give up, he remember something.

"The zodiac" Leo, said.

Maggie, look at him.

"Adrian was a gemini, lets look for air signs places" Leo said.

Maggie, got a map, they started looking.

Until Maggie, said.

"Here, a library, an old one"

Leo, agreed.

They have a place.

Armed with the new information gleaned from Adrian's diary – the "safe place" linked to air signs, and the old library – Leo and Maggie felt a renewed sense of purpose. They had a potential location, a place where Adrian might have hidden crucial evidence, a final message, perhaps even the key to stopping Albin Varga.

But before pursuing that lead, they decided to make one final attempt to extract information from Gregor Novotny. They had broken through his Capricorn defenses before, revealing his fear and his complicity in the conspiracy. Now, they needed to push him further, to see if they could get him to reveal the full extent of his knowledge, to confirm their suspicions about Albin Varga's ultimate plan.

The sleek, modern interior of Novotny Solutions felt like a battleground as Leo and Maggie entered. The employees, sensing the tension, moved with a heightened sense of caution, their eyes darting nervously towards Novotny's office.

Novotny greeted them with a forced smile, but his eyes betrayed a mixture of fear and resignation. He knew the game was up, that his carefully constructed world was crumbling around him.

"Detective Maxwell, Ms. Hart," he said, his voice strained, gesturing for them to sit. "I assume this isn't a social call."

Leo placed a single sheet of paper on Novotny's desk – a printout of Adrian's final diary entry, the one mentioning the "safe place" and his growing fear.

Novotny stared at the paper, his face paling, his hands trembling slightly. He recognized Adrian's handwriting, the desperate tone, the chilling premonition of his own death.

"Where... where did you get this?" he stammered, his voice barely a whisper.

"It doesn't matter," Leo replied, his voice cold and hard. "What matters is that we know about Adrian's fears, about his suspicions, about his... final message."

Maggie leaned forward, her voice sharp, cutting through the pretense. "We know about Albin Varga, Mr. Novotny. We know about 'Balance Keeper.' And we know about your... involvement."

Novotny's carefully constructed façade crumbled. He looked like a man who had been cornered, trapped, his secrets exposed.

"I... I told you," he whispered, his voice filled with a desperate, pleading fear. "I didn't have a choice. He... he made me do it."

"He made you help him murder Adrian?" Leo pressed, his voice relentless.

Novotny nodded slowly, his body shaking. "He said... he said it was necessary. That Adrian was... a threat. That he was going to... disrupt the balance."

"And what about this 'safe place'?" Maggie asked, her voice low and intense. "What did Adrian hide? Where did he hide it?"

Novotny hesitated, his internal struggle evident in his expression. He looked from Leo to Maggie, his eyes pleading for understanding, for help.

"I... I don't know," he whispered. "I swear. I don't know where it is."

Leo didn't believe him. He knew Novotny was still holding something back, still protecting someone, or something.

"Think, Mr. Novotny," Leo said, his voice firm and unwavering. "Adrian was a Gemini. He valued knowledge, communication, information. Where would he hide something important? Somewhere connected to those things."

Novotny's eyes flickered, a spark of recognition, a glimmer of understanding. He looked at Leo, then at Maggie, his expression a mixture of fear and... resignation.

"The... the library," he whispered, his voice barely audible. "The old... university library. He... he used to go there. To... to think. To... to research."

Leo and Maggie exchanged a look of grim understanding. The old university library. It fit. It was a place of knowledge, of information, of... secrets.

"What did he hide there, Mr. Novotny?" Maggie pressed, her voice urgent. "What was so important that Albin Varga was willing to kill for it?"

Novotny shook his head, his eyes filled with a chilling terror. "I... I don't know," he whispered. "He... he never told me. He just said... it was... the key. The key to... everything."

Leo stood up, his expression resolute. "Thank you, Mr. Novotny," he said, his voice cold and hard. "You've been... helpful." He knew Novotny was still withholding information, still protecting Varga, but they had what they needed. They had a location, a potential lead, a chance to finally uncover the full truth.

As they left Novotny Solutions, Leo felt a surge of adrenaline, a sense of impending confrontation. They were running out of time. Albin Varga was out there, somewhere, preparing to unleash his "Equilibrium Engine," to carry out his catastrophic plan. And they were the only ones who could stop him.

Maggie look at him.
"Let's get going" she said.
Leo, nodded

Chapter 21

The old university library, a towering gothic structure of stone and stained glass, stood in stark contrast to the modern, sterile environments of Novotny Solutions and Dvorak Technologies. It was a place of knowledge, of history, of secrets – and, Leo and Maggie hoped, the location of Adrian's "safe place," the repository of his final message.

As they approached the library, Leo felt a familiar prickling sensation on the back of his neck, a sense of unease, of being watched. He scanned the surroundings, his eyes searching for any sign of danger, any indication that they were not alone.

"We need to be careful," he said, his voice low and cautious, as they entered the building. "Varga knows we're closing in. He's likely to be... unpredictable."

Maggie nodded, her expression grim. "And Novotny... he's still out there. He might try to... interfere. Or... warn Varga."

The library was dimly lit, the air thick with the scent of old books and dust. The silence was almost deafening, broken only by the occasional creak of a floorboard, the distant rustle of pages. It was a place of quiet contemplation, of scholarly pursuit, but it also felt... oppressive, haunted by the ghosts of the past.

They began their search, moving slowly, deliberately, through the labyrinthine stacks of books, their eyes scanning the shelves, the tables, the hidden corners, searching for any clue, any hint of Adrian's presence, of his "safe place."

Leo, guided by his understanding of Adrian's Gemini personality – his love of knowledge, his curiosity, his need for communication – focused on areas that reflected those traits. He examined the reading rooms, the study carrels, the reference sections, searching for any sign that Adrian had spent time there, that he had left something behind.

Maggie, meanwhile, focused on the library's archives, on the older, less-frequented sections, on the hidden spaces where secrets might be concealed. She was looking for something out of place, something unusual, something that didn't quite fit.

Hours passed, and the library remained stubbornly silent, revealing nothing. The initial excitement of the search had faded, replaced by a growing sense of frustration, of disappointment.

It was Leo who finally made the discovery. While examining a section of books on astrology and the Zodiac – a seemingly unlikely place for Adrian to hide something of scientific importance – he noticed a small, almost imperceptible gap between two shelves.

He reached into the gap, his fingers brushing against something... cold, metallic. He pulled it out, his heart pounding in his chest. It was a small, locked box, made of steel, with a complex combination lock.

"Maggie," he said, his voice hushed, his eyes wide with a mixture of excitement and apprehension. "I think... I think I found it."

Maggie joined him, her expression mirroring his own. She examined the box, her fingers tracing the intricate design of the lock. "This is it," she said, her voice barely a whisper. "This is Adrian's safe place."

But the box was locked, and they didn't know the combination. They tried various combinations, dates, numbers, anything that might have been significant to Adrian, but nothing worked.

"We need to find the combination," Maggie said, her voice filled with a growing sense of urgency. "There has to be a clue... somewhere."

They returned to their search, this time focusing on the area around the bookshelf, on the books themselves, on any detail that might provide a hint, a clue to the combination.

Leo, remembering Adrian's Gemini nature, his love of puzzles, of riddles, of hidden meanings, began to examine the titles of the books on the shelf, searching for a pattern, a sequence, a code.

And then, he saw it. A series of numbers, subtly embedded in the titles of the books, a sequence that corresponded to the signs of the Zodiac.

Gemini – 3
Libra – 7
Aquarius - 11

"The air signs," Leo murmured, his voice filled with a sudden understanding. "He used the Zodiac... his own sign, Varga's sign... and... Aquarius." The sign of innovation, of rebellion, of... the future.

He quickly entered the combination into the lock: 3-7-11.

A click, a soft, almost imperceptible sound, and the box sprang open.

Inside, nestled on a bed of velvet, lay a single USB drive, and a handwritten note.

Leo picked up the note, his hand trembling slightly. It was addressed to him, and to Maggie.

"If you're reading this," the note began, *"it means I'm gone. It means Albin Varga has... succeeded. But it also means that you've found my safe place, that you've uncovered the truth. The USB drive contains all the evidence you need. Proof of Albin Varga's research, of his plans, of his... madness. It also contains... a warning. About the instability. About the... danger. Be careful, Leo and Maggie. You're dealing with forces you don't understand. And Albin Varga... he's not who you think he is. He's... something else. Something... more."* *

The note ended abruptly, unsigned.

Leo and Maggie exchanged a look of profound understanding. Adrian's final message, his warning, his legacy. They had found the truth, but the truth was far more complex, far more dangerous, than they had ever imagined.

Leo, grab the USB.

"Lets see what's inside" he said.

Maggie nodded.

THE CONTENTS OF THE USB drive, Adrian's final message, were a chilling confirmation of their worst fears. Albin Varga was not just a brilliant scientist with a distorted vision of balance; he was a dangerous, potentially unstable individual, capable of manipulating others and committing murder to achieve his goals.

Leo and Maggie spent hours analyzing the data on the drive, piecing together the final puzzle pieces of the conspiracy. They found detailed schematics of Varga's "Equilibrium Engine," complex equations outlining his theories on zero-point energy, and disturbing recordings of conversations between Varga, Novotny, and Dvorak.

"This is... terrifying," Maggie murmured, her voice hushed, her eyes fixed on the screen. "He's talking about manipulating the very fabric of reality, about creating a... a catastrophic event in order to... 'restore balance.'"

Leo nodded, his expression grim. "He's delusional," he said. "He believes he's acting for the greater good, that he's... saving the world. But he's... he's playing God. And he's willing to sacrifice anyone... anything... to achieve his goals." He thought of the Libra scales, tipped precariously towards darkness, towards chaos.

The recordings revealed the full extent of Novotny and Dvorak's complicity. Novotny, the pragmatic Capricorn, had provided the funding, the technology, the connections, driven by a desire for profit and power, but also, increasingly, by fear. Dvorak, the proud Leo, had provided the muscle, the influence, the willingness to eliminate obstacles, motivated by his own ambition and his misplaced trust in Varga's vision.

"They were both pawns," Maggie said, her voice filled with a mixture of anger and disbelief. "Varga was manipulating them, playing on their weaknesses, their ambitions, their... fears."

"And Adrian... he was the only one who saw the truth," Leo added, his voice filled with a profound sadness. "He was the only one who tried to stop him."

But the USB drive also contained something else: a detailed plan, a timeline, a location. Varga was preparing to activate his "Equilibrium Engine." He was planning to... "restore balance"... on a specific date, at a specific time, in a specific place.

"He's going to do it," Maggie whispered, her voice trembling with fear. "He's actually going to do it."

Leo's gaze hardened with resolve. "We have to stop him, Maggie," he said, his voice firm and unwavering. "We have to find him. And we have to stop him. Before it's too late."

They knew the final confrontation was imminent. They were running out of time. The scales of justice were tipping, and they were the only ones who could prevent the world from plunging into chaos.

They reviewed the location, a place outside Prague.

They had a place and a date.

Maggie, stood up.

"Let's get ready"

THE OLD UNIVERSITY library, their destination, was a place of shadows and whispers, a repository of knowledge and forgotten secrets. Leo and Maggie, armed with Adrian's final message, the cryptic combination, and the chilling contents of the USB drive, approached the building with a mixture of trepidation and determination.

They found the section indicated by Adrian's clue – air signs – and located the specific bookshelf. The small, steel box was still there, hidden in the gap between the shelves. Leo carefully entered the combination – 3-7-11 – and the box clicked open.

Inside, nestled on a bed of velvet, lay the USB drive and the handwritten note, just as they had seen before. But this time, they were ready to delve deeper, to understand the full scope of Adrian's discovery, of Albin Varga's plan, of the danger they faced.

They returned to Leo's office, the familiar clutter providing a strange sense of comfort in the face of the impending storm. They plugged the USB drive into Leo's laptop, the screen illuminating their faces with a cold, blue light.

The drive contained a wealth of information: detailed schematics of Varga's "Equilibrium Engine," complex equations outlining his theories on zero-point energy, research notes, simulations, and... recordings.

"Let's start with the recordings," Leo said, his voice low and serious.

Maggie nodded, her expression grim.

The first recording was a conversation between Adrian and Albin Varga, their voices strained, filled with a mixture of frustration and... fear.

"Uncle, you have to stop this," Adrian's voice said, his tone pleading. *"This is... it's too dangerous. You don't understand the... consequences."*

"I understand perfectly, Adrian," Varga's voice replied, cold and calm, filled with an unwavering conviction. *"I am restoring balance. I am... saving the world."*

"By destroying it?" Adrian countered, his voice rising in anger and disbelief. *"By unleashing forces you can't control?"*

"Control is an illusion, Adrian," Varga said, his voice smooth and patronizing. *"There is only... balance. And I... I am the instrument of that balance."*

The recording ended abruptly, leaving Leo and Maggie in stunned silence.

"He's... completely delusional," Maggie whispered, her voice filled with horror. "He truly believes he's doing the right thing."

"He's a Libra, Maggie," Leo said, his voice grim. "He's obsessed with balance, with harmony, with... justice. But his perception of those concepts is... twisted. He's lost sight of reality. He's... dangerous."

They listened to more recordings, each one more disturbing than the last. They heard Varga discussing his plans with Novotny, with Dvorak, manipulating them, exploiting their weaknesses, their ambitions, their fears. They heard Varga talking to himself, his voice filled with a chilling mix of scientific detachment and messianic fervor.

"The scales are tipping," Varga said in one recording, his voice echoing through the room. "The instability is growing. The time is... near. I must... I *will*... restore the equilibrium. Even if it means... sacrifice."

"He's planning to activate the engine," Maggie said, her voice trembling slightly. "He's going to... to do it."

"We need to find out where and when," Leo said, his voice firm with resolve. "We need to stop him."

They continued to analyze the data on the USB drive, searching for any clue, any detail, that might reveal Varga's plan, his location, his timeline.

It was Leo who made the final discovery. While examining the schematics of the "Equilibrium Engine," he noticed a small, almost hidden annotation, a set of coordinates, and a date and time.

"This is it," he said, his voice filled with a mixture of excitement and dread. "This is where he's planning to activate the engine. And... this is when."

He looked at Maggie, his eyes filled with a chilling certainty. "We're running out of time, Maggie. We need to go. Now."

He grabbed the files.

Maggie, followed him.

As they get to the door.

Leo, look at Maggie.

"Are you ready for this?"

Maggie, with a deep breath.

"Yes" she said.

Chapter 22

The coordinates extracted from Adrian's hidden USB drive pointed to a remote location outside Prague – an old, abandoned observatory perched atop a windswept hill. This was it, Leo knew: the place where Albin Varga planned to activate his "Equilibrium Engine," the place where he intended to "restore balance" to the universe, regardless of the cost.

The drive to the observatory was silent, filled with a palpable tension. The city lights faded behind them, replaced by the inky blackness of the countryside. The night sky, a vast expanse of stars, seemed to press down on them, a silent witness to the impending confrontation.

Leo gripped the steering wheel, his knuckles white, his mind racing. He thought of Adrian, of his brilliance, his fear, his desperate attempt to warn the world. He thought of Dvorak, the proud Leo, reduced to a pawn in Varga's game. He thought of Novotny, the calculating Capricorn, trapped by his own ambition and fear. And he thought of Albin Varga, the enigmatic Libra, the man who believed he could play God.

"He's a fanatic, Maggie," Leo said, his voice low and serious, breaking the silence. "He's driven by a belief, a conviction, that's beyond reason. He won't be swayed by logic, by appeals to morality, by... anything we might say."

Maggie nodded, her expression grim. "We need to be prepared for anything," she said. "He's already shown he's willing to kill. And he has... something. Some kind of weapon, some kind of... power." She shivered, remembering the chilling words from Varga's journal, the talk of harnessing zero-point energy, of manipulating the fabric of reality.

Leo glanced at her, his eyes filled with a mixture of concern and determination. "We'll face him together," he said, his voice firm. "We'll stop him. We have to."

As they approached the observatory, the silhouette of the building loomed against the night sky, a dark, imposing structure that seemed to exude an aura of menace. The wind howled around them, whipping their hair and clothes, adding to the sense of foreboding.

Leo parked the car some distance from the observatory, hidden amongst a cluster of trees. They didn't want to announce their presence, to give Varga any warning. They needed to approach cautiously, to assess the situation, to plan their next move.

"He's expecting us," Leo said, his voice barely a whisper, as they walked towards the observatory. "He knows we're coming. He's... prepared." He thought of the anonymous text messages, the cryptic warnings, the sense of being manipulated, of being led towards this final confrontation.

They reached the observatory's entrance, a heavy wooden door that stood slightly ajar, a sliver of darkness beckoning them inside. Leo drew his weapon, his senses on high alert, his body tensed for action. Maggie, her own hand resting on the pistol in her bag, stood close behind him.

He pushed the door open slowly, carefully, the creaking sound echoing through the stillness. The interior was dimly lit, illuminated by the faint glow of the moon filtering through the high, arched windows. The air was cold, heavy with the scent of dust and... something else. Something... metallic. Something... *electric*.

They stepped inside, their footsteps echoing through the silence. The observatory was a relic of a bygone era, filled with obsolete telescopes, astronomical charts, and strange, unidentifiable devices. It was a place of science, of observation, of... secrets.

And it was also, Leo knew, a place of danger. A place where a madman, driven by a twisted vision of balance, was preparing to unleash forces beyond human comprehension. A place where the scales of justice were about to tip, one way or another.

Leo, felt it.

The final part.

He look around.

"Stay close" he said to Maggie.

She got closer.

They were ready.

Inside the observatory, the air was thick with dust and the scent of decay, a testament to years of neglect. But there were also signs of recent activity: a high-powered telescope pointed towards the night sky, a table cluttered with notes and diagrams, and a faint, unsettling hum that seemed to emanate from the very walls of the building. This was Albin Varga's domain, a place where science and obsession had intertwined, creating something... dangerous.

Leo and Maggie moved cautiously through the observatory, their flashlights cutting through the darkness, their senses on high alert. They were searching for Varga, but they were also searching for... something else. Something that would explain his plan, his motives, his ultimate goal.

"He's trying to harness zero-point energy," Maggie murmured, her voice hushed, as she examined the notes on the table. "He believes he can... manipulate the fabric of reality, restore balance to the universe."

Leo nodded, his expression grim. "But his definition of 'balance' is... distorted. He's willing to sacrifice anything... anyone... to achieve his goals." He thought of the Libra scales, tipped precariously towards chaos, towards destruction.

They continued their search, moving through the maze of interconnected rooms, each filled with obsolete equipment and strange, unidentifiable devices. It was a place of forgotten science, of abandoned dreams, of a past that seemed to linger in the air like a ghostly presence.

It was in a small, cluttered room, filled with books on astrology and the Zodiac, that they found something unexpected: a series of photographs, pinned to a corkboard, depicting Albin Varga with various individuals, including Novotny, Dvorak... and Evan.

Leo felt a surge of adrenaline, a sense of... understanding. Evan, the secretive Scorpio, the one who had seemed so eager to deflect suspicion, the one who had claimed to have no knowledge of Adrian's project. He was *involved*. He was part of the conspiracy.

"He's been playing us all along," Maggie said, her voice filled with a mixture of anger and disbelief. "He's been... protecting Varga. He's been... part of the plan."

Leo nodded, his mind racing. He thought of Evan's Scorpio traits – his secrecy, his intensity, his... capacity for vengeance. Had he been motivated by loyalty to Varga? By a shared belief in his twisted vision of balance? Or by something else entirely?

Before they could delve deeper into this new revelation, they heard a sound – a faint, metallic click, followed by a low, humming noise. It was coming from the main observation dome, the heart of the observatory.

Leo and Maggie exchanged a look of grim understanding. Varga was there. And he was... activating something.

They moved quickly, silently, towards the dome, their weapons drawn, their bodies tensed for action. They reached the entrance, a large, circular opening that led into the vast, domed space.

And there, bathed in the faint glow of the moonlit sky, stood Albin Varga, his figure silhouetted against the backdrop of the high-powered telescope, his hands hovering over a complex control panel, his eyes fixed on the heavens.

He was... chanting, his voice low and resonant, a strange, unsettling mixture of scientific jargon and esoteric pronouncements.

*"The scales are tipping. The balance must be restored. The forces of chaos must be... contained." *

Leo and Maggie stepped into the dome, their presence breaking the spell, shattering the silence.

Varga turned towards them, his expression calm, almost serene, his eyes burning with an unnatural intensity. He seemed... unsurprised to see them.

"Detective Maxwell, Ms. Hart," he said, his voice smooth, almost welcoming. "You've found me. But you're too late. The process has already begun."

He turned to the machine.

"The time for justice is now." he said.

Leo and Maggie, got closer, guns pointed at him.

They were there.

The observatory dome felt less like a scientific sanctuary and more like a ritual chamber. Albin Varga stood before his "Equilibrium Engine," a silhouette against the backdrop of stars, the unsettling hum of the machine a constant, throbbing presence. The air itself felt charged, heavy.

"You've been busy, Detective Maxwell, Ms. Hart," Varga said, his voice carrying an unnervingly smooth quality, almost a purr. It lacked any trace of nervousness, any hint of fear. "Following the threads, unraveling the web... I must say, I'm impressed. Few have come this far." He still hadn't turned to face them.

"We know about 'Balance Keeper,' Mr. Varga," Leo replied, his voice level, betraying none of the turmoil he felt inside. His hand rested near his weapon, but he made no move to draw it. Not yet. "We know about Adrian, about Dvorak, about Novotny. We know about *you*."

Varga chuckled softly, a sound that scraped against Maggie's nerves like sandpaper. "You know *nothing*," he said. "You see the shadows, the surface ripples, but you don't comprehend the depths. You don't understand the... *necessity* of my work."

"The necessity of murder?" Maggie challenged, her voice tight with controlled fury. The memory of Adrian, his brilliance extinguished, fueled her defiance.

Varga finally turned, his eyes, reflecting the faint starlight, seemed to gleam with an unnatural intensity. "You speak of justice, Ms. Hart? Of morality? Such... limited concepts. Such... *human* concerns." He took a step towards them, his movements fluid, almost graceful. "I am concerned with a far greater balance, a cosmic equilibrium that transcends your petty notions of right and wrong."

Leo felt a cold knot in his stomach. This wasn't the detached pronouncements of a scientist; this was the self-assured rhetoric of a zealot. "What gives *you* the right to decide what that balance is?" Leo asked, keeping his voice even, trying to engage Varga, to understand the twisted logic that drove him.

Varga's lips curled into a faint smile. "The universe itself, Detective Maxwell. The laws of physics, the fundamental forces that govern all of existence. They are... out of alignment. And I... I am the only one who can restore them."

"By destroying everything?" Maggie's voice was sharp, cutting through Varga's pronouncements.

Varga's gaze shifted to Maggie, a flicker of something that might have been annoyance crossing his face. "Destruction is merely a prelude to creation, Ms. Hart. A necessary... recalibration. Think of it as... pruning a tree. Sometimes, you must remove the diseased branches to allow for healthy growth."

Leo felt a surge of anger, but he forced himself to remain calm. He needed to keep Varga talking, to understand the scope of his plan, to find a weakness. "And Adrian? Was he a 'diseased branch'?"

Varga's expression hardened. "Adrian was... misguided. He lacked the vision, the understanding, to appreciate the... necessity of my work. He became... an impediment." He spoke of his nephew with a chilling lack of emotion, as if he were discussing a faulty piece of equipment.

"He was your *family*," Maggie repeated, her voice laced with disgust. She couldn't comprehend this level of detachment, this cold-blooded justification for murder.

"Sentimentality is a luxury we can no longer afford," Varga said, his voice taking on an edge. "The stakes are too high. The future of... everything... depends on my success."

Leo shifted his weight slightly, his muscles tense. He could feel the hum of the machine growing stronger, the air growing heavier. He knew they were running out of time. "What exactly are you planning to do, Varga?"

Varga turned back towards his machine, a strange, almost ecstatic light in his eyes. "I'm going to restore balance, Detective. I'm going to... realign the fundamental forces. I'm going to... usher in a new era."

He reached out towards the control panel, his fingers hovering over a series of buttons and switches. The humming intensified, vibrating through the floor, through their very bones.

Maggie, her reporter's instincts screaming at her, took a small step forward. "What will that *do*?" she asked, trying to keep her voice steady, trying to buy them time.

Varga glanced back at her, a flicker of impatience in his eyes. "It will... correct the instability. It will... cleanse the universe of its imperfections. It will..." He paused, a strange smile playing on his lips. "...create a new beginning."

Leo knew they couldn't wait any longer. He subtly signaled Maggie.

This was their moment.

Leo slowly, moved closer to Varga.

THE WAREHOUSE WAS A cavernous, echoing space, filled with the ghosts of past transactions, of illicit deals, of secrets kept hidden in the shadows. It was here, amidst the dust and the decay, that Leo and Maggie planned to confront Novotny and Dvorak, armed with the evidence from the USB drive and a desperate hope that they could finally unravel the truth.

As they waited, hidden in the shadows, they heard the sound of approaching vehicles, the crunch of tires on gravel, the murmur of voices. Novotny and Dvorak had arrived, their alliance, their partnership, about to be tested in the crucible of their shared guilt.

Leo and Maggie stepped out of the darkness, their sudden appearance startling the two men. Novotny, ever the controlled Capricorn, recovered quickly, his expression shifting to a mask of cold defiance. Dvorak, the proud Leo, seemed to shrink, his usual confidence replaced by a flicker of fear.

"Detective Maxwell, Ms. Hart," Novotny said, his voice smooth but laced with an undercurrent of tension. "To what do we owe this... unexpected pleasure?"

Leo ignored the sarcasm, his gaze fixed on the two men. "It's over," he said, his voice firm and unwavering. "We know about 'Balance Keeper.' We know about Adrian's murder. And we know about your... collaboration."

He held up the USB drive, the small device containing the damning evidence. "We have proof, gentlemen. Proof of your involvement, of your guilt."

Dvorak's composure cracked. He looked at Novotny, his eyes filled with a mixture of fear and accusation. "You said... you said we wouldn't be caught," he stammered. "You said... it was foolproof."

Novotny turned on Dvorak, his expression furious. "You fool!" he snapped. "You were the weak link. You were the one who panicked."

"I panicked?" Dvorak retorted, his voice rising in anger. "You were the one who orchestrated everything! You were the one who..."

Leo stepped forward, his voice cutting through their argument. "Enough!" he said, his tone sharp and commanding. "We're not here to listen to you blame each other. We're here for the truth. And we're going to get it, one way or another."

He turned to Dvorak, his gaze unwavering. "You admitted to orchestrating Adrian's sabotage, Mr. Dvorak. But you claimed you didn't kill him. Is that still your story?"

Dvorak hesitated, his eyes darting nervously between Leo and Novotny. He was trapped, caught between his fear of the law and his even greater fear of his former partner.

"I... I didn't want him dead," he finally whispered, his voice barely audible. "I just... I wanted him silenced. I wanted him to stop... interfering."

"But he didn't stop, did he?" Maggie said, her voice filled with a mixture of sadness and anger. "He kept digging. He kept searching for the truth. And that's why he was killed."

Dvorak looked down at his hands, his expression a mixture of shame and regret. "I... I didn't know... I didn't realize... how far it would go," he stammered.

"Who gave the order, Dvorak?" Leo pressed, his voice relentless. "Who told you to kill Adrian?"

Dvorak looked up, his eyes meeting Leo's, a flicker of fear in their depths. "It... it wasn't Novotny," he said, his voice barely a whisper. "It was... someone else."

"Who?" Maggie asked, her voice sharp with urgency.

Before Dvorak could answer, Novotny stepped forward, his expression a mixture of anger and desperation. "Don't listen to him!" he said, his voice rising. "He's lying! He's trying to shift the blame!"

"I'm not lying!" Dvorak retorted, his voice filled with a desperate plea. "It was... it was *him*. He's the one who... who gave the order. He's the one who... who controls everything."

"Who, Dvorak?" Leo pressed, his voice low and intense. "Tell us! Who is the mastermind behind all of this?"

Dvorak hesitated, his eyes darting around the warehouse, as if searching for an escape route. He looked at Novotny, his expression filled with a mixture of fear and hatred. Then, he looked back at Leo, his eyes widening in terror.

"It's... it's..." he stammered, his voice barely a whisper. He opened his mouth to speak, to reveal the name, to finally expose the truth.

But before he could utter a single word, a shot rang out, echoing through the cavernous space. Dvorak gasped, his eyes widening in shock and pain, his body convulsing as he clutched at his chest.

He crumpled to the ground, his lifeblood staining the dusty concrete floor.

Leo and Maggie reacted instantly, drawing their weapons, their eyes scanning the shadows, searching for the shooter. But the warehouse was silent, empty, the only sound the echo of the gunshot and the ragged breathing of the dying man.

They had been so close. So close to uncovering the full truth, to exposing the hidden mastermind. But now, their key witness was dead, silenced forever, and the scales of justice had tipped once again, plunging them back into the darkness, leaving them with more questions than answers.

Leo, knelt down, and check Dvorak's pulse.

He look up to Maggie.

With a sad tone he said.

"He is gone"

Maggie, frustrated.

"Who did this?, Who shot him?"

Leo, stood up.

"We need to find out, and fast"

Chapter 23

The drive to the observatory was a tense, silent journey. Dvorak's confession, and Novotny's subsequent breakdown, had confirmed their darkest fears: Albin Varga was the true mastermind, and his "Equilibrium Engine" was a threat of unimaginable proportions. The city lights faded behind them, replaced by the stark, unforgiving beauty of the night sky.

"He's planning to activate it tonight," Maggie said, breaking the silence, her voice tight with apprehension. "Adrian's notes... the coordinates... the timeline... it all points to tonight."

Leo gripped the steering wheel, his jaw clenched. He could feel the weight of responsibility pressing down on him, the knowledge that they were the only ones standing between Varga and his catastrophic plan. "We know he's obsessed with balance, with this twisted idea of cosmic equilibrium. But what does that *mean*? What's he actually going to *do*?"

Maggie shook her head, her brow furrowed in thought. "I don't know. His research is... it's beyond anything I've ever encountered. He's talking about manipulating fundamental forces, about harnessing energy sources that... that shouldn't even be possible."

As they neared the observatory, the building's dark silhouette rose against the star-studded sky, an ominous presence dominating the landscape. It looked less like a place of scientific inquiry and more like a temple to some forgotten, dangerous god.

Leo parked the car a considerable distance away, concealed behind a thick stand of trees. They would approach on foot, minimizing the risk of detection.

"He'll be expecting us, or at least, someone," Leo said, his voice low, as they prepared to leave the car. "He knows we've been investigating. He knows we're close." He checked his weapon, the cold steel a reassuring weight in his hand.

Maggie adjusted the strap of her bag, her hand instinctively moving to the pistol inside. "He's not a soldier, Leo," she said, her voice betraying a hint of uncertainty. "He's a scientist. He might be... unpredictable."

Leo met her gaze, his expression grim. "He's a fanatic, Maggie. Driven by an obsession. And he's willing to kill to achieve his goals. That makes him more dangerous than any soldier." He thought of the Libra scales, of the delicate balance between reason and madness, and how easily that balance could be shattered.

They moved towards the observatory, their footsteps silent on the soft earth, their senses on high alert. The wind whispered through the trees, carrying with it the scent of pine and... something else. Something... metallic. Something... *charged*.

The observatory's main door was unlocked, ajar, as if inviting them in. Leo hesitated, his hand hovering over the doorknob. He exchanged a look with Maggie, a silent communication of shared apprehension and determination.

He pushed the door open, the hinges groaning in protest, the sound echoing through the stillness. The interior was dimly lit, illuminated by the faint glow of the moon filtering through the high, arched windows. The air was cold, heavy with the scent of dust and... that strange, metallic tang.

They stepped inside, their bodies tensed, ready for anything. The observatory was a relic of a bygone era, filled with antiquated telescopes, dusty astronomical charts, and strange, unidentifiable devices. It was a place of science, of observation, of... secrets.

And it was also, Leo knew, a place of immense danger.

They moved slowly, cautiously, their flashlights cutting through the darkness, their eyes scanning the shadows, searching for any sign of Albin Varga, any indication of his presence, of his plan.

The silence was broken only by the creaking of the building, the rustling of unseen things, and... a faint, persistent hum. A hum that seemed to be growing stronger, more insistent, with each passing moment.

"He's here," Leo murmured, his voice barely a whisper. "And he's... activating something."

They followed the sound, their footsteps muffled by the thick layer of dust on the floor. It led them to the main observation dome, the heart of the observatory, where a massive, high-powered telescope stood pointed towards the night sky.

And there, bathed in the ethereal glow of moonlight, stood Albin Varga, his figure silhouetted against the backdrop of the stars, his hands hovering over a complex control panel, his eyes fixed on the heavens. He was muttering to himself, his voice a low, rhythmic drone, a strange, unsettling blend of scientific jargon and esoteric pronouncements.

Leo took a breath.

Maggie, prepare herself.

They were there.

Leo took a deep breath, trying to quell the surge of adrenaline that threatened to cloud his judgment. He needed to remain calm, to think strategically. This wasn't a simple arrest; it was a confrontation with a man who believed he held the fate of the world in his hands.

"Mr. Varga," Leo said, his voice level, projecting authority without aggression. "We understand you believe you're acting for the greater good. But you're mistaken. You're playing with forces you don't comprehend, and you're putting countless lives at risk."

Varga's gaze remained fixed on the control panel, his fingers twitching slightly. "You cannot possibly understand," he said, his voice a low, almost hypnotic murmur. "The universe is out of balance. It *must* be corrected."

Maggie stepped slightly to the side, subtly positioning herself to provide cover for Leo while also getting a better view of the control panel. She tried to make sense of the array of dials, switches, and glowing displays, searching for any indication of what Varga was about to do, any clue as to how to stop him.

"Adrian understood," Maggie said, her voice challenging, hoping to provoke a reaction, to break through Varga's detached demeanor. "He understood the danger. That's why he tried to stop you."

Varga finally turned his head, his eyes focusing on Maggie with a chilling intensity. "Adrian was... misguided. He lacked the vision. He clung to... outdated notions of morality, of... consequence."

"He clung to life," Leo countered, his voice hardening. "He valued human life, something you seem to have discarded in your pursuit of... what? Cosmic balance?"

Varga's lips curled into a faint, almost pitying smile. "Such limited perspectives," he said. "You cling to the microcosm, while I am concerned with the macrocosm. The survival of... everything." He turned back to the control panel, his fingers resuming their delicate dance over the buttons and switches.

The humming sound intensified, vibrating through the floor, through their very bones. Leo felt a growing sense of unease, a prickling sensation on his skin. He knew they were running out of time.

Instead of a direct, physical confrontation, Leo decided to try a different approach. He needed to disrupt Varga's focus, to shake his confidence, to create an opening. He remembered Dr. Horáková's words: "He's not himself anymore." He had to reach whatever remained of the *man* beneath the madness.

"Professor Varga," Leo said, his voice taking on a new tone, one of... respect, almost deference. "Your research... it's truly groundbreaking. The concepts you're exploring... they're revolutionary."

Varga paused, his fingers hovering over the control panel, his head tilting slightly, as if listening to a distant sound. A flicker of... vanity?... crossed his face.

"You... understand?" he asked, his voice losing some of its cold detachment.

"I'm trying to," Leo said, carefully choosing his words. "But... there's something I don't quite grasp. This... 'instability' Adrian was so worried about. Can you... explain it to me?"

Varga turned slightly towards Leo, his eyes narrowing. He seemed to be considering the question, weighing the risks of revealing his secrets against the... lure of recognition, of appreciation. The Libra, craving validation, even now.

"It's... complex," Varga said, his voice hesitant. "But... in essence... the universe is expanding at an accelerating rate. This expansion is creating... a strain. A... tear... in the fabric of reality."

"And your engine... it can fix that?" Maggie asked, her voice carefully neutral, playing along with Leo's strategy.

Varga nodded, a spark of pride in his eyes. "It can... realign the forces. It can... restore the balance. It can... prevent the catastrophic collapse of... everything."

Leo saw his opportunity. He subtly shifted his weight, preparing to act, while keeping his voice calm and even. "But... what if you're wrong, Professor? What if your calculations are... flawed? What if, instead of restoring balance, you... accelerate the collapse?"

Varga's eyes widened, a flicker of doubt, of fear, crossing his face. It was a fleeting moment, but it was enough.

Leo lunged. Not towards Varga, but towards the control panel. He had seen enough of the schematics, enough of Adrian's notes, to have a *general* idea of the machine's workings. If he could just...

Varga reacted instantly, his Libra composure shattered. He turned, his hand reaching out towards Leo, a strange, almost desperate expression on his face.

But he was too late.

Maggie Moved.

The air inside the observatory dome crackled with an unnatural energy. Leo and Maggie stood their ground, flashlights illuminating Albin Varga's gaunt figure. He was older, more frail in appearance than his photographs suggested, but his eyes burned with an unsettling intensity. The humming of the "Equilibrium Engine" was a constant, throbbing presence.

"Albin Varga," Leo said, his voice level, projecting authority. "We know about 'Balance Keeper.' We know about Adrian. It's over."

Varga gave a chillingly soft chuckle. "Over? Detective, it's only just *beginning*. You have no conception of the forces at play, the delicate balance that I alone can restore."

"Balance by murder?" Maggie challenged, stepping slightly forward, her voice edged with controlled anger. "By manipulating people like Dvorak and Novotny? By unleashing something you can't possibly control?"

Varga's gaze shifted to Maggie, a flicker of something unreadable in his eyes. "Sacrifices are necessary, Ms. Hart. Collateral damage in the grand scheme of things. Adrian... he was becoming a liability. He understood too much, yet not *enough*."

"He understood enough to know you were insane," Leo countered, subtly adjusting his stance, preparing for any sudden movement from Varga. He needed to keep him talking, to understand the full scope of his plan, to find a weakness. "What *is* this 'instability' he was so worried about? What were you *really* working on?"

Varga gestured towards the complex array of machinery surrounding the telescope. "Zero-point energy, Detective. The energy of the vacuum itself. Limitless. Clean. And... volatile. Adrian discovered a flaw, a... resonance cascade... that could occur if the energy flow wasn't perfectly calibrated."

"And you ignored him," Maggie said, her voice tight with accusation.

"He lacked vision!" Varga snapped, his composure momentarily cracking, revealing the fanatic beneath. "He saw only the danger, not the potential. I can *control* it. I can *harness* it. I can *use* it to... rebalance the universe." His eyes took on a distant, almost dreamy quality. "To correct the errors of creation."

Leo, using his understanding of the Libra archetype, decided to try a different approach. "Professor Varga," he said, his voice softening slightly, adopting a tone of... almost respect. "Your research... it's truly remarkable. The concepts you're exploring... they're revolutionary. But... what if there's a flaw in your calculations? What if, instead of restoring balance, you... trigger the very catastrophe Adrian feared?"

Varga turned his gaze back to Leo, a flicker of uncertainty, of... doubt... crossing his face. It was a fleeting moment, but Leo seized upon it.

"Adrian was a brilliant scientist, Professor," Leo continued, pressing his advantage. "He was your nephew. He cared about you. He wouldn't have warned you without reason."

Varga's hand, which had been hovering over the control panel, trembled slightly. "He... he didn't understand," he stammered. "He couldn't see the... the bigger picture."

"Show us, then," Maggie interjected, her voice firm but not aggressive. "Show us the bigger picture. Explain it to us. Help us understand."

Varga hesitated, his internal struggle evident. The desire for recognition, for validation – a classic Libra trait – warred with his obsession, his paranoia, his... madness.

For a moment, it seemed as if he might actually comply. He took a step towards them, his eyes losing some of their feverish intensity.

But then, the humming of the machine intensified, the air growing thick with a strange, electric charge. Varga's gaze snapped back to the control panel, his expression hardening, his resolve returning.

"It's too late," he said, his voice cold and devoid of emotion. "The process has begun. The balance... will be restored."

His hand moved towards a large, red button on the control panel.

Leo knew they couldn't wait any longer. He shouted, "Maggie!", a prearranged signal.

Maggie reacted instantly. She lunged forward, not towards Varga, but towards the side of the control panel, where, based on Adrian's notes and diagrams, a secondary power conduit was located.

Varga, distracted by Maggie's sudden movement, turned his head, his eyes widening in alarm. It was the opening Leo needed.

He didn't draw his weapon. He knew that a gunshot, in this confined space, with this volatile machinery, could have catastrophic consequences. Instead, he launched himself at Varga, tackling him around the waist, driving him away from the control panel.

They crashed to the floor, a tangle of limbs and struggling bodies. Varga, despite his age, was surprisingly strong, fueled by his fanaticism and desperation. He fought back with a ferocity that belied his frail appearance.

Maggie, meanwhile, reached the side of the control panel. She quickly located the power conduit, a thick bundle of cables feeding into the machine. Without hesitation, she ripped the cables apart, severing the connection.

The humming sound abruptly ceased. The lights flickered, then died, plunging the observatory dome into darkness.

Varga screamed, a sound of pure, unadulterated rage and despair. "No! You fools! You don't understand what you've done!"

Leo, struggling to subdue Varga, managed to get a pair of handcuffs on him. He pulled the struggling scientist to his feet, his grip firm.

"It's over, Varga," Leo said, his voice breathless but firm. "You're finished."

Varga, his body slumping in defeat, looked up at Leo, his eyes filled with a mixture of hatred and... something else. Something that looked almost like... relief.

"You haven't won," he whispered, his voice barely audible. "You've only... delayed the inevitable. The scales... will tip. The balance... *will* be restored."

As the police sirens wailed in the distance, growing closer, Leo felt a profound sense of exhaustion, of relief, but also... of unease. He had stopped Varga, he had prevented the immediate catastrophe, but he knew that the larger questions, the deeper mysteries, remained. The anonymous texts, the cryptic warnings, the sense of being manipulated... it all pointed to something... more.

Maggie placed a hand on his arm, her touch a silent reassurance. "We did it, Leo," she said, her voice soft but firm. "We stopped him."

Leo nodded slowly, his gaze fixed on the now-silent machinery, on the defeated figure of Albin Varga. He had won this battle, but he knew the war was far from over.

Epilogue

The arrest of Albin Varga and the dismantling of "Balance Keeper" made international headlines. The details of Varga's research, his "Equilibrium Engine," and his plan to "restore balance" were deemed too dangerous for public release, classified at the highest levels.

Gregor Novotny, facing overwhelming evidence and the collapse of his carefully constructed world, cooperated fully with the authorities, providing further details about Varga's operation and his own role in the conspiracy. He received a reduced sentence in exchange for his testimony.

Albin Varga, deemed mentally unfit to stand trial, was confined to a secure psychiatric facility, his research confiscated, his dreams of cosmic balance shattered. He remained convinced of his own righteousness, a tragic figure consumed by his own delusions.

Leo and Maggie returned to their lives, forever changed by their experience. They had faced darkness, had stared into the abyss, and had emerged victorious. They had brought a measure of justice to Adrian Varga and had prevented a potential catastrophe.

One evening, a few weeks after the case had been closed, Leo and Maggie sat on Leo's balcony, overlooking the city of Prague. The night sky was clear, the stars shining brightly, a silent testament to the vastness and mystery of the universe.

"Do you ever wonder," Maggie asked, her voice thoughtful, "if Varga was right? About the universe being out of balance, I mean."

Leo considered her question, his gaze fixed on the stars. "Perhaps there's a truth to his theories," he said, "a grain of reality within his madness. But... balance isn't something you impose. It's something you... strive for. Something you... find. In yourself, in your relationships, in the world around you."

He looked at Maggie, a faint smile touching his lips. He'd found a balance he hadn't anticipated, a partnership that grounded him.

Maggie smiled back. She reached for his hand, their fingers interlacing.

"Ready for the next case?" Leo asked, a hint of challenge in his voice.

Maggie squeezed his hand. "Always," she replied, her voice filled with a quiet confidence. The city lights twinkled below them, a vibrant tapestry of life, a reminder that even in the darkest of times, there was always hope, always the possibility of finding balance, of finding justice, of finding... connection. And as long as they had each other, they could face whatever the future held.

Weeks after the dust settled – after Albin Varga was deemed unfit to stand trial and confined, after Novotny began his long sentence, and after the details of "Balance Keeper" were buried under layers of government classification – Prague returned to its normal rhythms. The city buzzed with life, tourists thronged the Charles Bridge, and the Vltava flowed on, seemingly indifferent to the darkness that had briefly threatened to engulf it.

For Leo Maxwell, however, the world felt irrevocably changed. The immediate danger was past, but the echoes of the case lingered – not as shadows, but as lessons learned, as scars that served as reminders of the fragility of balance and the enduring power of human connection.

He found himself drawn back to the old university library, the place where Adrian had hidden his final message. He wandered through the familiar stacks, the scent of old books and aged paper a strange comfort. He paused at the bookshelf where they had found the hidden box, running his hand along the spines. He could almost picture Adrian there, seeking solace amidst the knowledge contained within those volumes.

He wasn't searching for anything specific, just... reflecting. Trying to make sense of the events, of the motivations, of the madness that had driven Albin Varga. He thought about the Zodiac, about the archetypes, about the ways in which people's inherent natures could be both their greatest strength and their greatest weakness.

As he stood there, he noticed something he hadn't seen before: a small, almost imperceptible inscription on the underside of the shelf, just above where the box had been hidden. It was a single word, written in a delicate, almost faded script: *Forgiveness*.

Leo stared at the word, his heart aching with a mixture of sadness and understanding. *Forgiveness*. Was it Adrian's message to his uncle? A plea for understanding? Or was it a message to himself, a reminder to forgive his own perceived failings, his inability to prevent the tragedy? He realized it was all of those things, and more. Justice wasn't just about punishing the guilty; it was about finding peace, about finding forgiveness, both for others and for oneself. It was about finding a balance within, a way to move forward, to carry the weight of the past without being consumed by it. He thought of his sister, and for the first time in a long time, the sharp edges of his guilt seemed to soften, replaced by a quiet sense of... acceptance.

He left the library, the word *forgiveness* echoing in his mind, a guiding principle, a path towards healing.

One evening, he met Maggie at their usual café. He didn't tell her about the inscription, not yet. It was something he needed to process, to fully internalize, before he could share it.

They sat in comfortable silence for a while, sipping their drinks, watching the city lights flicker on as darkness descended. The tension of the past few weeks had finally dissipated, replaced by a sense of... quiet contentment, a shared understanding that transcended words.

"I've been thinking," Maggie said, breaking the silence, her voice thoughtful. "About Varga, about his obsession with balance. About... what it all means."

Leo nodded, his gaze fixed on the swirling steam rising from his coffee cup. "Me too," he said. "It's... a complex question. Is the universe inherently balanced? Or is it constantly striving for equilibrium? And what's our role in all of this?"

Maggie hesitated, then offered, "Maybe... maybe it's not about finding a perfect, static balance," she said. "Maybe it's about... accepting the inherent imbalance. About finding a way to live with the chaos, the uncertainty, the... imperfections. About finding balance *within* ourselves, even when the world around us is... unbalanced."

Leo looked at her, a faint smile touching his lips. "Maybe you're right," he said. "Maybe that's the key. To find our own center, our own equilibrium, even amidst the storm." He reached across the table and took her hand, his fingers interlacing with hers. It was a simple gesture, but it spoke volumes. It was a connection forged in danger, strengthened by shared experience, by mutual respect, by... something more.

"Thank you, Maggie," he said, his voice filled with a quiet gratitude. "For... for everything."

Maggie squeezed his hand, her eyes meeting his, a silent understanding passing between them. "Thank you, Leo," she said. "For... for being you."

A few days later, Leo received a package. Inside was a leather-bound journal, its cover embossed with a constellation map. Beneath it lay a note written in Maggie's familiar handwriting:

"For the next mystery—and the next. May the stars always guide you."

He smiled, tracing the constellations with his finger. He opened the journal to the first page, where Maggie had added another message:

"Justice begins with understanding. Keep looking to the stars. And keep looking out for each other."

Leo sat down at his desk, pen in hand, the journal open before him. He thought of Adrian, of his brilliance, of his tragic end. He thought of Varga, of his madness, of his twisted vision of balance. He thought of all the others who had been caught in the web of deceit – Dvorak, Novotny, Evan, Lukáš. He thought of his sister. And he thought of Maggie.

He took a deep breath and began to write. Not about the case, not about the details, but about the *lessons*. About the importance of forgiveness, of acceptance, of finding balance within oneself. About the enduring power of human connection, of partnership, of hope.

He knew the world was full of mysteries, full of darkness, full of injustice. But he also knew that there was light, there was hope, there was the possibility of finding balance, of finding peace, of finding... justice. And he, armed with his knowledge, his intuition, his experience, and his partnership with Maggie, was ready to face whatever the future held. The stars might guide, but it was up to them to choose their path, to navigate the complexities of human existence, to strive for a better world, one case at a time. He wasn't just a detective for hire anymore; he was a seeker of truth, a champion of balance, a guardian of justice. And he wouldn't rest until the scales were, as much as they could be, set right. He closed his eyese, took a deep breath and smiled.

Don't miss out!

Visit the website below and you can sign up to receive emails whenever Daniel Sanjurjo publishes a new book. There's no charge and no obligation.

https://books2read.com/r/B-A-WQHBB-LPVBG

BOOKS 2 READ

Connecting independent readers to independent writers.

Did you love *Justice in the Shadows*? Then you should read *A Life Concealed*[1] by Daniel Sanjurjo!

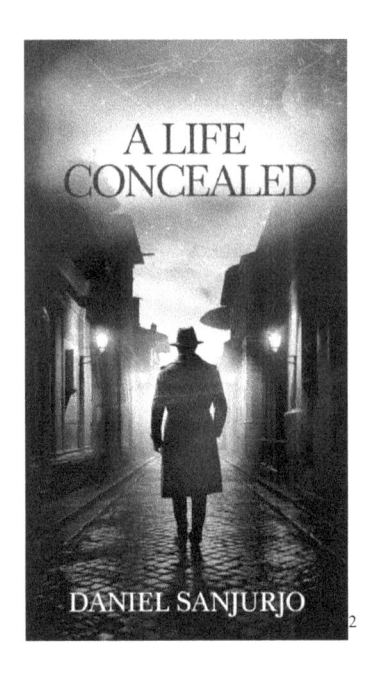

When Clara Reeves hires Leo Maxwell to investigate her father's death, she knows something the police refuse to see — Arthur Reeves didn't take his own life. In a world where power silences truth, Leo's unconventional methods become Clara's last hope.

Guided by a blend of intuition and the zodiac, Leo navigates a labyrinth of secrets inside the Reeves family's world of wealth and privilege. As the trail leads him from the shadowy streets of Rome to the cold halls of London high

---

1. https://books2read.com/u/4A0VMo

2. https://books2read.com/u/4A0VMo

society, Leo must untangle a web of hidden alliances, betrayals, and lies — all while haunted by the ghosts of his own past.

A Life Concealed is a slow-burn detective mystery where human nature holds the key to unlocking the truth — if you know where to look.

Also by Daniel Sanjurjo

101 Astrology
The Complete Guide to Astrology

Birthdays Profiles
The Secret Language of Birthdays Profiles - January Personality Insights.
The Secret Language of Birthdays - February Personality Insights
The Secret Language of Birthdays March Profiles
The Secret Language of Birthdays April Profiles
The Secret Language of Birthdays For May

The Zodiac Detective
The Zodiac Detective Under the Sign of the Killer
Tide of Lies
A Life Concealed
Justice in the Shadows

Zodiaco
Aries 2024 Mes Por Mes
Tauro 2024 Mes Por Mes
Géminis 2024 Mes Por Mes
Cáncer 2024 Mes Por Mes
Leo 2024 Mes Por Mes:
Virgo 2024 Mes Por Mes
Libra 2024 Mes Por Mes
Escorpio 2024 Mes Por Mes
Sagitario 2024 Mes Por Mes
Capricornio 2024 Mes Por Mes
Acuario 2024 Mes Por Mes
Piscis 2024: Un Viaje Celestial
Piscis 2024 Mes Por Mes

Zodiac world
Aries Revealed 2024
Taurus 2024
Leo 2024
Gemini 2024
Cancer horoscope 2024
Virgo 2024
Scorpio 2024
Sagittarius 2024
Capricorn 2024
Aquarius 2024

Standalone
Cosmic Revelations 2024
Dreams Interpretation Guide
Explorando Mis Sueños: Descubre el Mundo Fascinante de tu Mente Nocturna
Moon And Astrology Planner 2024
Numerology 101 Beginner's Guide to Numerology
An Apologetic Journey: Exploring Christianity

www.ingramcontent.com/pod-product-compliance
Ingram Content Group UK Ltd.
Pitfield, Milton Keynes, MK11 3LW, UK
UKHW040827130325
456214UK00001B/4